Isado

Isadora Elzbeth

Caroline Barry

ATTIC

First published in 1999 by Attic Press
Attic Press
Crawford Business Park
Crosses Green
Cork
Ireland

British Library Cataloguing in Publication Data
A CIP catalogue record for this book is available from the British Library.

ISBN 1 85594 194 5

Cover illustration by Philippa Gossage
Typeset by Red Barn Publishing, Skeagh, Skibbereen, Co. Cork
Printed by ColourBooks Ltd, Baldoyle, Co. Dublin

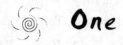# One

It all began with a murder of crows…

Isadora Elzbeth looked at the crows.

'Murder,' she whispered, and the crows lifted their heads and turned to look at her. She was fourteen years old, small for her age, with long curly dark hair and smoky-grey eyes. She was dressed in black. She held a lemonade bottle in her pale hands and sipped at it through a straw.

The crows moved towards her, on their spiky thin legs, waiting in a semi-circle around her black patent shoes.

'Murder,' she whispered again, slowly raising her right hand and pointing to a grim, coffin-shaped cloud that stretched over the pine trees. The crows turned their heads and all at once they flapped up into the air, cawing furiously at the wind. Isadora Elzbeth blinked as they moved like an unfurling cloak towards the trees. She frowned when one crow broke away from the rest and flew back to her. His beak was a thick grey wedge, which opened and closed.

He craked:
'Isadora Elzbeth,
There is a globe and an apple
And a star that is a snake,
Isadora Elzbeth
Go in search of death.'

His wide wings flapped close to her face and his beak was menacingly close to her nose.

'He could have easily bitten it off and flown away with it,' she told Penguin later. 'I swear I thought I saw white pearly teeth inside his beak.' Penguin rolled his eyes to heaven. He took most things that Isadora Elzbeth said with a grain of salt.

The crow flew away, laughing as it disappeared over the trees, leaving Isadora Elzbeth standing alone in the garden staring at the far distant sea.

Mrs. Buck found her and whispered into her ear, as if to speak out loud might shatter Isadora Elzbeth into a thousand tiny pieces.

'Darling, you must come inside now, out of the weather.'

Isadora Elzbeth had wanted to say that there was nothing wrong with the weather, and that she'd much prefer to stay out in the garden away from all the strange faces gathered in her kitchen. She hardly knew any of the people who had swarmed into the house. Quite frankly she hated the way everyone looked so pityingly at her. Everyone moved slowly and spoke secretively, sipping tea or nibbling at triangular-shaped sandwiches, then shaking their heads and telling each other it was 'tragic'. Isadora Elzbeth just wanted them all to go away, to put everything back where they had found it, to put on their coats and to leave by the front door. But she didn't say any of this, except to Penguin, and that was much later, when they were alone together.

'Isadora Elzbeth, it's almost time to go.' Mrs. Buck's voice was like custard, creamy and yellow. Of all her mother's friends, Isadora Elzbeth liked her the best. She wore outrageous dresses and always had unusual handbags. Today Mrs. Buck wore a black dress that was disappointingly sombre.

'Not one of her usuals,' Isadora Elzbeth thought, then she said it out loud, because she felt she should.

'Black doesn't suit you, Mrs. Buck. Why didn't you wear your pink dress?'

Mrs. Buck's eyes filled with water and Isadora Elzbeth suddenly realised she'd made a terrible mistake.

'Oh God, Mrs. Buck, don't cry. You don't look at all ugly, it's a nice dress, it's just that it's boring. Everyone else is wearing black and you just normally never dress like everyone else. Don't cry, Mrs. Buck, it's only a dress. It's only my opinion, don't listen to me, what do I know about clothes?'

Mrs. Buck was weeping uncontrollably into a soggy tissue when Penguin passed by and told Isadora Elzbeth to stop talking.

'For God's sake, you can't be upsetting the neighbours like this,' he chided. 'Offer her some lemonade, see if that will stop her crying.'

Mrs. Buck didn't wait to be offered, she reached out and took the bottle from Isadora Elzbeth. She sucked a big chunk out of the drink, dabbed her eyes and took a deep breath.

'We have to go soon, darling,' she said with her custardy voice. 'You can bring Penguin with you if you like. Would you like me to sit with you in the limousine?'

Isadora Elzbeth nodded. She took Mrs. Buck's hand and was led back into the house, where all the people were gathered in serious groups, tutting and sighing and turning to look and stare silently as they passed by.

The limousine was long and black and shiny. Isadora Elzbeth thought it looked like a giant insect. She sat beside Mrs. Buck, who carefully fastened the safety belt for Penguin. The driver wore a black hat and gloves. He said nothing. The limousine pulled out of the driveway and slowly proceeded along the country road. Everybody else got into their own cars and followed. Isadora Elzbeth wanted to tell the driver to put his foot down, to try and lose them, but she knew there was nothing he could do. Outside the window the world passed slowly by. Everything seemed to approach the car in a stately fashion. Distant trees drew near, bowing elegantly. The faraway sea waved in. Enormous boulders of grey granite crept down onto the road and leaned back as the car drove by. Bulrushes and wild bogland stopped moving to turn around and look as Isadora Elzbeth passed by.

'The world is different from inside a car, isn't it, Mrs. Buck?'

But Mrs. Buck was sipping on a bottle of gin, oblivious to everyone.

'What's a globe, Mrs. Buck?' Isadora Elzbeth had to touch Mrs. Buck's hand to make her listen.

'A globe?' Mrs. Buck's eyes widened at the question. Her face looked slightly looser; the gin had washed away her coral lipstick and made her cheeks burn.

'Oh darling, why do you want to know about a globe?'

'Because I think I have to find one.'

Mrs. Buck lit a cigarette. 'It's a model of the planet earth. Like a football with a map of the world on it.'

Then, slipping an arm around Isadora Elzbeth's shoulders, she offered to buy her one. Isadora Elzbeth had wanted to say, 'Well I know that definition of a globe. I just wondered if there were other globes, if the word had other meanings.' But she didn't, instead she remained quiet.

They didn't speak again until the limousine pulled into the churchyard and drew to a halt outside the church door.

'What will happen to me now?' Isadora Elzbeth asked, but Mrs. Buck collapsed into tears and muttered something indecipherable to the priest who had come to shake their hands.

Isadora Elzbeth didn't cry once. She felt too cold inside to cry, too horrified to think about it. She walked behind the coffins to the graveyard. She threw a white rose on her father's coffin and a red rose on her mother's. She watched them being lowered into the ground and paid no attention when people came to her and said that *mammy and daddy are with the angels now.* She tried to believe that they were dead, but somehow she thought it might be an elaborate practical joke, that they were going to pop out from behind a tree, laughing and shouting, 'It's only a trick.' But they never did.

Isadora Elzbeth was an orphan. She looked at all the gravestones and thought about all the people lying beneath them, and then she wondered what the crow had meant when he said *Isadora Elzbeth, go in search of death.* And then she thought she had a headache, so she stopped thinking about everybody who was buried underground and tried to find Mrs. Buck, who had wandered off somewhere to have another cigarette. Isadora Elzbeth found Mrs. Buck sitting beneath a cherry blossom tree. Her eyes were puffy and sad, but she pretended to be happy.

'Well, little orphan,' she smiled, 'you want to know what will happen to you?' Isadora Elzbeth settled down beside her and nodded. 'How would you feel about living in Dublin?'

There was no answer to this, so Mrs. Buck explained.

'I have a friend. She's an old friend of your mother's. Emigrated to Spain many years ago. She moved back recently. Rents a very nice flat in the city. She's a painter, and I've been on the telephone to her, and she said that she would very much like it if you and Penguin would come to visit for a while. What do you think?'

Isadora Elzbeth shrugged her shoulders. She'd never been to the city. She'd never met this painter friend of her mother's, though she did remember foreign envelopes arriving in the post. She knew she couldn't stay at home in her own house, because it would feel too empty, so she agreed to pack her bags and tell Penguin they were leaving Blessing Hill to go to Dublin city.

Two

Mrs. Buck insisted on being called **Marian**. She arrived down in the kitchen the next morning wearing a short, flowy, see-through dress of blue flowers. Underneath she wore a tight dark dress that hinted at curves and exotic femininity. She unbolted her large square handbag and produced a packet of cigarettes. For a small woman she smoked a lot.

'Christina is baking meringues for tea.' Realising that this made no sense, Mrs. Buck explained. 'At 30 Wexford Street, in Dublin city. The woman we're going to visit, I phoned her this morning and she said she was baking meringues especially for the occasion. Her name is Christina. An excellent painter.' Mrs. Buck's chocolate-brown eyes paused in mid-distance. She was conjuring up paintings of seas and towers, of night birds and desolate boglands. Isadora Elzbeth stood perfectly still and waited for Mrs. Buck to return from wherever she was inside her head.

'An excellent painter,' Mrs. Buck whispered, 'but doomed.' The words rolled out like a slow, heavy fog and struck Isadora Elzbeth as being very strange.

'Marian, what do you mean *doomed?*'

'Oh,' Mrs. Buck shook the cobwebs away, 'did I say doomed? I didn't mean that. She's not a successful artist, that's what I meant, financially that is. Her paintings are considered old-fashioned, figurative. She refuses to paint what she calls "abstract splodges" just to be part of the avant-garde circle. She's a very feisty woman. She once punched a man in the eye because he talked such rubbish about art.' Mrs. Buck laughed, a warm, relishing laugh.

'I think you'll like Christina.' Then, changing the subject altogether, she snapped open her handbag and produced a flat box and a bag of toffee bonbons. She popped a bonbon into her mouth and rustled the little white bag under Isadora Elzbeth's nose. They looked at each other and chewed on the sweets for a while, then Mrs. Buck handed over the flat box before drifting out into the garden to look at the tulips.

The flat box had a sticker on it with a picture of a blue world surrounded by bold writing: SHARDAN'S INFLATABLE GLOBE.

Isadora Elzbeth was delighted. When Penguin wandered into the kitchen he found her puffy-cheeked and red in the face blowing into a blue ball.

'When are we going to Dublin?' he asked.

Isadora Elzbeth pinched the white air bracket and took little panting breaths.

'Don't talk to me now, Penguin. Can't you see I'm blowing up the world.'

When the operation was completed she held out the globe and admired the light blue seas and the different-coloured continents printed on it. Penguin was not impressed. He wiggled his ears and looked out of the window at Mrs. Buck walking among the tulips.

'You know, for a cat you're not very curious,' Isadora Elzbeth complained. 'You're indifferent, that's what you are, an indifferent cat.' She tucked the globe under her arm and marched upstairs to get her moth collection.

It was a difficult relationship to explain. Isadora Elzbeth and Penguin were inseparable. They both talked to each other, but only occasionally understood what the other said, since one spoke only English and the other only ever said 'meow'. Penguin had a better grasp of English than Isadora Elzbeth had of cat language. But Isadora Elzbeth was convinced that there was deep meaning behind Penguin's language. He seemed an intelligent cat, he could suck lemonade through a straw. Once or twice she found him walking on his hind legs, and she would never forget the Tuesday evening she caught him doing handstands up against the pear tree. Moments like that were precious.

Their friendship was cemented by beautiful misunderstandings. For example, at the end of every lunar cycle, Isadora Elzbeth and Penguin both wandered down to the bottom of the garden to watch the full moon rise. While they sat watching, up out of the grasses and from deep among the trees, a myriad of tiger moths shimmered in the pale light, all of them desperately trying to reach the moon, their wings gently beating, their small eyes hopelessly attracted to the bright satellite circling the earth. Then Isadora Elzbeth sang to the moths, sweet melancholy tunes. Penguin howled up at her to 'Give over, please stop, can't you shut up? Can't you just look at them without whining?' But to Isadora Elzbeth it was all 'meows', to her Penguin was joining in. In his tuneless cat way she thought he was singing too. Then she'd slip her arm around his furry shoulders, 'That's right, Penguin, sing!' And he'd sigh. 'Oh, what's the use,' he'd say, before shoving his head up into her armpit to see if that would distract her.

Mrs. Buck heard Isadora Elzbeth talking to herself. 'We'll never again sit under the pear tree by the river. We'll never say *don't the moths look like tiny kites*, because there are no moths in the city. Moths are allergic to neon light.'

'Who are you talking to?' Mrs. Buck asked, making Isadora Elzbeth jump about two feet into the air with fright.

'God, Marian, I thought you were the wardrobe talking.'

They both laughed at that idea and Mrs. Buck settled down on the bed to look at the sketchbook spread over it. It was Isadora Elzbeth's sketchbook, filled with drawings of some of the moths she had collected. Azure-blue moths with brown furry bodies and long antennae were boldly drawn in soft pastels. Grey moths with dark markings were drawn beside common scaly-winged ones. Rare pink-flamed specimens glowed beside African whites. All of them were named and numbered. 'Angel', No: 186. 'Cavalier', No: 3. 'Blue Puff Willow', No: 76. Mrs. Buck was very impressed.

'Yes,' she said approvingly, 'I think you will definitely like Christina.'

Then she leapt off the bed as though she'd been struck by a bolt of electricity.

'It's eight-thirty,' she announced, suddenly panic-stricken. 'We'd better go, or we'll miss the train.'

An unusual wave of misery gobbled up Isadora Elzbeth. She looked bleakly around her bedroom. All her books and posters and toys seemed to reach out to her – her army tent set up in the corner, her binoculars, her writing desk that when she was younger she sometimes turned over and pretended was a ship. She was leaving all these things behind. But she didn't cry. She buttoned up her green coat, picked up her sketchbook and her globe, said a quiet goodbye to her gossamer net and empty jar and walked behind Mrs. Buck, who was carrying her suitcase out to the car. Old Jack was to give them a lift to the station.

As they pulled out of the driveway Isadora Elzbeth couldn't look back. She couldn't watch her home shrink away and disappear behind her. She couldn't bear the idea of its being empty and alone. And she half imagined that, if she did look back, the windows and doors would suddenly open and shout at her to come home. So she stared straight ahead, looking at the world outside the windscreen and listening to Mrs. Buck telling fantastic stories about Dublin.

Three

The train looked like a long orange caterpillar. Mrs. Buck settled in at the window seat and smiled at Isadora Elzbeth as she sat opposite. There was a table in between them, and Mrs. Buck placed her handbag on it and snapped open the gold clasp. She began shuffling around inside it, looking for something, while at the same time explaining to Isadora Elzbeth.

'Christina gave the key to me, I'd swear it.'

She began emptying out the contents of her bag onto the table. There were lipsticks and pens, a smooth circular powder compact with a painted rose on one side and an eye that blinked on the other. Notebooks and three purses, a silver chain, some shells and a chunk of rough pink stone.

'You can never find anything when you want it. I bet it's the last thing . . . Aha!'

Mrs. Buck slowly withdrew her hand from the jaws of her handbag. Between her forefinger and her thumb she had a yale key. She held it in mid-air as though it were some rare artefact that should be looked upon solemnly.

'The key to 30 Wexford Street.'

Isadora Elzbeth nodded politely. She wanted to say, 'It's a door key, Marian, let's not get too carried away.' But instead she opted for bouncing her head up and down affirmatively while Mrs. Buck seemed to drift off into a world of her own.

'I remember the parties. The pink gin and the poker games. I used to borrow Christina's dresses. We'd stroll around Stephen's Green and have scones and coffee in the Shelbourne Hotel. We felt so refined. Then at night we'd meet up with friends in a tiny wine bar on South Anne Street and just natter the night away. We'd talk about books and paintings and joke sarcastically at anyone who took it too seriously. But that was a long time ago, before Christina went away, before she was ill, before Gabriel came.'

Mrs. Buck turned to look out of the window. Her skin was clear and delicate, she wore no make-up except for a slash of crushed plum lipstick. Her brown hair curled slightly beneath her ears and accentuated the long line of her jaw. Her fringe was out of fashion, but Mrs. Buck wore it so well. Her smooth brown eyes turned to look at Isadora Elzbeth.

'What would you like to do in Dublin?' she enquired.

Undaunted, Isadora Elzbeth ignored the question.

'Who's Gabriel?' she asked, 'and why did everything change after he came?'

Mrs. Buck seemed pleased. She smiled and lit a cigarette with such panache that it made Isadora Elzbeth want to smoke.

'You don't miss a trick. No flies on you, heh! We called him the Archangel. He just turned up on the scene one evening. In a dark-grey suit. He sat in the corner, and had the arrogance to stare at us. But, you've got to understand, he was extremely handsome. He had jet-black hair and continental-coloured eyes, black as olives. He had a rugged jaw and a masculine forehead and the audacity to stare at us while we sipped wine and laughed. He was the worst kind of man . . . Mysterious.' Here Mrs. Buck began to frown. It was an intelligent frown, the kind that tries to figure something out.

'We ignored him that night, but we studied him as he left. He was a tall man, with broad shoulders, but not too well-built. He moved gracefully without swaggering. I thought he was vain. He disappeared out of the door and Christina turned to me and declared she was in love. I laughed and laughed. "It's typical of you," I said. "Go ahead and fall in love with dark strangers, but don't expect me to pick up the pieces when he breaks your heart." And that's exactly what she did. She fell in love with the Archangel. That winter Christina turned into something beautiful. Her hair glistened with health, her eyes flashed with optimism, she was effervescent. On the third evening in the wine bar Gabriel introduced himself. He gazed unashamedly at Christina and she flirted outrageously with him. She began painting again, she had been going through a bad phase and had produced no work for some time. Now she was inspired. But the strange thing was, while Christina was never happier, her paintings were becoming more odd. They were getting darker, sadder. Her colours captured less light, they exuded deep sorrow. She painted desolation and loneliness, twisted and agonised landscapes. It was as though she was trying to capture silence She had a solo exhibition that spring. I jokingly called it "the graveyard sideshow". It opened on the day the clocks were due to go forward. I remember the long stretch in the evening light. We toasted with Bollinger champagne and showed off our best dresses and generally flounced about the place, flitting from conversation to conversation. There were speeches and applause. Red dots appeared all over the walls, the paintings were selling like hot cakes. It was a roaring success. But as the evening wore on Christina seemed agitated. She smiled less, she looked anxiously through the crowd towards the door. I can still see how expectant she was with each new person who came in. She was looking for Gabriel, her Archangel. He never came. He vanished. Disappeared into thin air, never to be heard of again. One day he was there, the next day he was gone, without explanation. Men!'

Mrs. Buck sucked on her lips and shook her head.

'Christina recovered, because Christina is strong. But if I could catch the man myself I'd beat him to a pulp for breaking her heart the way he did. Still, at least she could

17

paint again, beautiful mysterious paintings.' Then she very bluntly asked, 'Have you any intention of falling in love?'

Isadora Elzbeth sat up straight and wondered about the idea.

'No, Marian, I can honestly say I have no intention of falling in love.'

Mrs. Buck was very satisfied. She explained how love was very tricky and fairytale-ish and not at all easy to find. And how it was much better to enjoy one's own company than to have to suffer the company of a mundane man. 'But,' she added with a wicked twinkle in her eye, 'if you do find love, proper love that is, well, together you can turn the world inside out and upside down and laugh at all the confusion.' And then, contradicting herself out of all proportion, she concluded that 'true love is not always romantic'.

Isadora Elzbeth saw her mother and father kissing in the garden, but she destroyed the memory, pushing it far away inside her head and closing it shut with a blink of her eyes.

'Will I have my own room in Dublin?' she asked worriedly, 'and will Christina mind Penguin sharing with me?' Mrs. Buck assured her that anything she wanted to do she could do, that Christina was very relaxed. She promised to stay for a while in Dublin to help Isadora Elzbeth settle in and suggested that they go to afternoon tea in the Shelbourne Hotel the next day by way of a special treat.

The train wiggled its way into Heuston station and hissed to a shuddering halt. Penguin, who had slept for most of the journey, stuck his head up over the table and balanced his chin on it.

'I'm hungry,' he moaned. He glanced up at Isadora Elzbeth. 'Corrh, that woman doesn't half talk. Archangels and love and painting. I have a headache listening to her. Can I have some sardines?'

Isadora Elzbeth translated his speech.

'He says thank you very much, Marian, for the train journey, he really enjoyed it.'

Mrs. Buck looked sceptically into Penguin's round smirking face and then stunned him by saying, 'I have some sardines in my bag. You can have them as soon as we get to the flat.'

Penguin sat up alert, his ears pricked the air, there was more to Mrs. Buck then he had previously thought. He was on his guard and his best behaviour as they stepped off the train and into a taxi.

It was three o'clock in the afternoon and the traffic was heavy. Isadora Elzbeth gazed out of the window, and the walls of the Guinness brewery stared flatly back at her. The car twisted out into the traffic. Grey and red-bricked buildings with dark empty windows leaned in to take a look at her as the car passed by. They drove over a bridge and up along the quays. The streets were busy, filled with people criss-crossing each other, stopping at traffic lights, turning to go into shops, half-halting to talk briskly to each other before dashing on. Isadora Elzbeth suddenly felt like she was in a pot of grey soup and all the people were ingredients being stirred by a large invisible spoon. She got a quick ache in her heart. If only she could curl up under-neath her pear tree and listen to the grass rustle. She did not like the city one bit. Everything was brick and stone and not at all like home.

When the taxi stopped it wasn't in a nice part of town. It pulled up outside a butcher's shop which had the name 'Hogans' written up over it. Beside the butcher's shop there was a dingy black door with the number 30 screwed into it. Isadora Elzbeth's heart sank; it looked unloved. Mrs. Buck bounced out of the taxi and shouted in to the man with the beard behind the butcher's counter.

'Hiya, Christy. How are you keeping?'

Christy came out and shook her hand. He smiled warmly as he was introduced to Isadora Elzbeth, but he welcomed Penguin with a suspicious eye.

'I think she's up there,' Christy said as Mrs. Buck twisted the key in the lock and pushed the black door open.

As soon as they stepped inside, Isadora Elzbeth wanted to cry. The hallway was falling apart – paint crumbled off the walls and strips of old wallpaper curled and peeled away in gluey patches. It was dark and gloomy. Penguin couldn't resist saying, 'Cod! Couldn't you have taken us somewhere more seedy?' But Mrs. Buck's glare shut him up. They climbed the rickety staircase and all that Isadora Elzbeth could think was that she had left home to come and live in a tenement. She wanted to turn around, go to her own house and fall into her mother's arms, but she wouldn't let herself think about that.

They mounted flights of stairs and turned onto a landing lit by a broken window. A gust of cold wind threateningly lifted the grimy curtain that covered it. Even Mrs. Buck seemed to shudder. On the second floor there was a pale green door, with a curled up cardboard picture of Jesus dangling from the gas pipe above it. Mrs. Buck knocked on the door and pushed it open confidently.

'We're here,' she called out cheerfully as she stepped into a stunning red hallway and led the way through to a white room that was ablaze with light and flowers. Paintings, framed in pale gold, hung like magical openings on the walls. It was an octagonal-shaped room and in the centre was a table laid with fine bone china and chocolate-oozing cream cakes and meringues. Standing by the window in the afternoon light was an extraordinary looking woman. She had silver-grey hair, yet her face was open and young. Her eyes were a flash of blue glass, her lips were a shiver of pink, spread into a broad, welcoming smile. Isadora Elzbeth was dazzled and surprised. This was not what she had expected to find.

Four

Christina flittered forward. Her feet were bare.
'At last,' she beamed, 'you've all arrived. It's good to see you.'

She swept towards Mrs. Buck and embraced her with long, flowing arms, then she took a steady, kind look at Isadora Elzbeth.

'How incredibly Gothic you look. Isn't she extraordinary, Marian? Her eyes. Isadora Elzbeth, you are most welcome and so is your furry companion. Your cat can do whatever he likes, but he can, under no circumstances, use my brushes.'

Everyone smiled politely at this idea, because no one thought for a second that Penguin would want to paint.

'As if!' Penguin replied, but under Mrs. Buck's stare added, 'Thanks for the welcome and all.'

'Well come on, come on.' Christina bounced towards the table and encouraged everyone to sit down and eat. Sunlight poured into the room, it gleamed off the bone white china and flashed on the knives that lay crossways over starched white napkins. Christina poured steaming hot tea into each cup, even Penguin's, and handed round the tiered cake stand of sumptuous cream cakes and meringues. Her good humour was infectious. Isadora Elzbeth felt so comfortable that she had no qualms about tying a napkin around Penguin's neck so that he wouldn't crumb his front with flakes of pastry.

'Doesn't she look like Catherine Earnshaw?' Christina said to Mrs. Buck and, without waiting for an answer, she continued. 'You look like the girl in *Wuthering Heights*. Did you ever hear of that book?'

Isadora Elzbeth shook her head.

'Catherine Earnshaw was an elfish looking thing just like you. Dark and passionate. There's a gypsy somewhere in your blood. Perhaps on your father's side,' she suggested.

Isadora Elzbeth remembered her father, tall and slender, chopping wood in the garden. She turned her face towards her plate and tried not to look sad.

'She's not mentioned them,' Mrs. Buck whispered to Christina. 'I think perhaps it's *post traumatic stress disorder.*'

The last part of this sentence faded off into a mime on Mrs. Buck's lips. Both women looked sympathetically towards each other and then the conversation broke away onto another subject.

'Have you organised it yet?' Mrs. Buck asked over the

rim of her snow-white cup. There was a flicker of mischief in her eyes.

'Well it just so happens, Marian, that I almost have. Operation "Scarlet" will soon be finished and then we shall head up, up and away!'

Mrs. Buck giggled. 'I cannot believe you're going to do it, Christina.'

'In the name of art, damn right I am! I am going to out-publicise Handley, if I can. And if that means stealing thunder, then that's what I will do.'

Penguin screwed up his cat face and swallowed back a chunk of chocolate icing.

'What are you two women talking about?' he meowed. 'Up, up and away to steal the thunder!'

'I'm going to fly,' Christina answered, causing Penguin to momentarily choke on the new mouthful he was swallowing. The last thing he needed was another woman who understood him.

'It's a competition between me and an old enemy of mine, Johannes Handley. He's an installation artist, he welds piles of steel together and calls it art. Don't get me wrong, he's an extremely good sculptor, but I like to provoke him when I can, keep him on his toes, so he doesn't lose his edge. You know, I once gave him a fat black eye, but that's another story. He has a new show opening up in the Irish Museum of Modern Art. His new work is wonderful, but he has given the show a very long pretentious title: *I am Scarlet and Airborne. What is your reply?* That's the title! I joke you not. I mean, what does it mean?' The question flashed in Christina's blue eyes, there was a hot blush on her cheeks. She threw back her head and laughed. 'It means a golden opportunity for fun, that's what it means!'

Mrs. Buck looked towards Isadora Elzbeth and leaned close to her.

'Art is not always about expression, sometimes it's about downright jealousy.'

Isadora Elzbeth laughed merrily, but she hadn't a clue what the women were talking about. She was getting a headache from desperately trying to keep track of the conversation.

'I've got a balloon!' Christina suddenly announced. 'Yes I have, a hot-air balloon, and very conveniently it is made from scarlet sailcloth. See, *scarlet and airborne*. We can travel to the exhibition opening in it, all of us. It will be amazing fun. Handley will be so disgusted, he may even try to shoot us down.' Christina and Mrs. Buck were in hysterics of laughter. 'What an entrance! Handley will hate to be out-dramatised.'

'Marian,' Isadora Elzbeth quietly asked, 'isn't that stealing his limelight?'

The two women howled with laughter.

'They're bloody mad,' Penguin mumbled to himself, 'bloody mad.'

Christina and Mrs. Buck were wrapped in animated conversation. Arriving at the show in a scarlet hot-air balloon was a brilliant idea. But what about the rest of the title to his show, *What is your Reply?* How would they answer Johannes Handley's question. They could reply by

25

throwing something down out of the balloon. They played with the idea of throwing flour and eggs, but Mrs. Buck suggested that this was perhaps a bit coarse and that they should consider throwing down something more sophisticated and cryptic as a counter-challenge. Both women explored this plan, which to Isadora Elzbeth seemed horribly childish and stupid, and anyway, from where she sat, it looked as though they were going to sabotage his big night, which seemed very unfair.

She wanted to sneak off into a corner with Penguin and sleep for a bit, it was all too dizzy and headache making in Dublin. She went very quiet, until finally Christina noticed she wasn't speaking.

'You must be tired from your journey, little Wuthering girl. Let me show you your room, then you can unpack.'

Christina stood up. The sun slowly withdrew from the room, sucked away by a grey cloud. She slipped her feet into gold Chinese slippers and picked up an enormous key from the mantelpiece.

'The key to the castle,' she said smiling as she led the way out through the two doors and back into the musty stairwell. She glanced along the grimy walls up to the floor above and quietly began climbing the stairs.

'This way,' she whispered and Isadora Elzbeth felt scared. Penguin bounced up onto her shoulders and hid himself beneath her dark thick curls. His pink nose sniffed the damp, mildewed air. He whispered, so the other two couldn't hear, 'They're strange, Isadora Elzbeth, very very strange,' but it all sounded like 'meow' to her.

The stairs creaked and heaved as they climbed them. Strips of linoleum curled loose from ancient tacks. Mouse holes were gnawed into the skirting-board. They passed another grubby window. Christina turned onto the third-floor landing and stopped outside a faded white door. Its one remarkable feature was an enormous gilded lock.

'The key to the castle,' she repeated, before placing the large ornate key into the lock and turning it. There was a clunk. For a split second Isadora Elzbeth thought she heard a startled scream, then a pattering like small feet on wooden floorboards. There was a scuffle and a small thud that for all the world sounded like a little door slamming. Penguin jumped down and looked quizzically under the door jamb with one eye. He could distinguish nothing, only a spider making what looked like candyfloss in the corner.

Christina pushed the door open, and a dusky light slipped out of the room.

'I'd best open the curtains,' she said.

Isadora Elzbeth followed her. She couldn't believe what she had stepped into. Her eyes swished around, trying to take it all in. This was no ordinary room. It was like a magical castle whirling with curiosities. There were gold mirrors, ornate lamps, amazing pictures that hung along the walls from the ceiling to the floor. There was a walnut wardrobe in the shape of Cinderella's carriage. A Victorian fireplace, decorated with red-and-white tiles, protruded from the odd-shaped corner at the edge of the room. There was an old desk covered with interesting looking

27

bric-a-brac. Dark leather books were piled on the floor. An ancient brass telescope was positioned at the long window. The window itself was extraordinary. It stretched from the floor to the ceiling, and it consisted of two plain sheets of glass that could be opened outwards. But perhaps the most beautiful thing of all was the bed. It was a four-poster, small and gorgeous, covered with blue velvet and surrounded by festoons of tissue-soft muslin that draped elegantly to the floor. An exotic landscape was painted on the headboard. Isadora Elzbeth was impressed.

'This is your room,' Christina announced. 'I do hope you like it, Wuthering girl. You can put your clothes in here.'

She opened the wardrobe and a dozen red butterflies fluttered out of the door, their soft wings disturbing the dusty air. Mrs. Buck laughed and opened her bag.

'Christina! How long has this place been locked up? There are butterflies nesting here!'

One by one the butterflies disappeared into the soft silk lining of Mrs. Buck's handbag. Isadora Elzbeth wondered how Marian could do that, but Christina didn't seem to notice the butterflies being captured.

'I use this room every evening, Marian. Well, OK, I pass through it to get to the roof. There's only one of me and there are only so many places I can be at the one time.'

As the last red admiral zigzagged its way into Mrs. Buck's handbag, Christina flung open the window and stepped out onto the sill. Penguin screamed hysterically, 'Don't do it, don't do it!' But it was too late, Christina had jumped, and even Mrs. Buck looked momentarily alarmed. Instead of hearing the heart-wrenching scream and the horrible splat of Christina's body plunging through the air to the ground beneath, they heard an animated command.

'Well, come on and see.'

Mrs. Buck jumped out of the window. Penguin looked hopelessly around him.

'Let's escape,' he howled, but Isadora Elzbeth thought that he wanted to be carried, so she wrapped her arms around him and stepped up onto the sill. There was a drop of about one foot onto a slender balcony.

'Scaredy cat!' Isadora Elzbeth whispered, relieved that she wasn't going to have to fling herself down from a three-storey building. She jumped onto the balcony. A brick wall covered with ivy hemmed her in from the height beneath. She didn't look directly down, instead her eyes scanned the distance. She could see the ruins of a walled garden and a cluster of neglected trees. Somewhere above her she heard voices.

'Cooee.' Isadora Elzbeth looked up and there was Mrs. Buck peeping over the brim of the roof, her chocolate-coloured eyes bronzed by the sunlight. 'Come on up,' she said, pointing further along the balcony to a flight of narrow steps. 'Wait until you see what is up here!'

Isadora Elzbeth let Penguin cling to her back. She didn't understand that he was screaming frantically at her to turn around and take him inside. Her pale hands firmly gripped the banisters and, with each step she took, Isadora

Elzbeth felt like she was climbing into the sky. When she arrived on the roof Christina waved and called, 'This is it. Come on, there's plenty of room, come on inside.'

Mrs. Buck and Christina were standing in an enormous basket that was surrounded by a swell of scarlet balloon cloth. Isadora Elzbeth made her way over to them, gingerly stepping around the scarlet cloth. She climbed inside and took a good look around. She'd never seen a roof garden before. The basket was hemmed in by garden furniture, there was a lily pool with a sparkling fountain and plants in brightly coloured pots. Beyond the roof the view was spectacular. Handsome chimneys tapered elegantly into the sky. Gulls and starlings swooped overhead, needle-thin aerials rose up out of roofs. And way down below, the streets twisted and curved like a miniature map. The city looked like a web of slender lines and the human beings looked like trapped insects.

'What will become of me?' Isadora Elzbeth quietly asked herself, but all she heard was Christina chattering on.

'We'll wear eighteenth-century costumes, just for the hell of it, and masks. Maybe I'll bring the telescope to look through as we travel, and some champagne to toast the voyage.'

Mrs. Buck pulled a compass out of her handbag and Isadora Elzbeth began to wonder about the two women. They were unusual. Looking at them now, she realised their eyes had the same expression. A metallic, sparkly light emanated from them. They spoke over and at each other, and they giggled an awful lot. In fact both women were downright *girlie*. It was all very tiresome but what could she do? She had to join in with all the silliness, otherwise where would she sleep? Who else was there to look after her? The day had been too long and too strange. Dublin was too big and too noisy. Christina and Mrs. Buck were two dizzy birds. 30 Wexford Street was too creepily grubby and too creepily unfamiliar. It was infested by tiny creatures who scuttled behind the skirting-boards. There was nothing peaceful or still about the place. She had no mother or father to calm her worries away. Suddenly Isadora Elzbeth dissolved into tears. She wanted to sob underneath the pear tree at the bottom of her garden. She buried her head in her hands and wept, vaguely aware that Penguin had nuzzled his nose between her fingers and was soothingly licking her tears away.

'Hush,' Christina said, gently wrapping her arms around her. 'There, there, let it all out, sweetheart.'

Isadora Elzbeth couldn't help it, she felt so lonely she wanted to lie down and sleep for a million years and never wake up. How could her mother and father have died, and left her without saying goodbye? How could they forget her just like that? It was unforgivable. Penguin embraced Isadora Elzbeth's head and squashed her face to his furry white belly.

'Shush now,' he crooned, 'we'll go to bed early. We'll have some hot chocolate and marshmallows and go to bed early.'

Mrs. Buck and Christina agreed that this was a good idea.

'It's been too much for one day,' Mrs. Buck said, producing a wad of pink tissues from her handbag. 'The sun is setting anyway. Let's all go inside.'

The first star of evening popped out through the twilight. The red-hot sun was going down, streaks of red and dark blue ran along the western horizon. One by one, the neon orange streetlights flickered on. One by one, people made their weary way home through the dreary city streets.

Once inside, Christina lit a fire in Isadora Elzbeth's bedroom. Mrs. Buck began unpacking the small tartan case. Penguin jumped up and down on the bed to test it and Isadora Elzbeth changed into her long nightdress. After that they sipped hot chocolate and adjusted the height of the lamp so that Isadora Elzbeth could turn it off while she was lying in bed. They shifted bits of furniture into new and better positions and brought in Isadora Elzbeth's sketchbook and her inflatable globe. They looked at the moon through the telescope and Christina sang an old Spanish song that had a pretty tune. Then it was time to say goodnight. Mrs. Buck kissed Isadora Elzbeth's forehead. She smelled of crushed apples and whiskey and when she stood up to leave the room she seemed to teeter slightly to one side.

'Don't worry, wildling,' she said, 'things can only get better.'

Christina waved as she slipped out of the door. 'Leave the light on all night if you like,' she said before she disappeared, 'and if you need me, just call.'

Five

They were gone. Isadora Elzbeth heard them going down the stairs. A door slammed beneath her, then, up through the floorboards, she heard the distant sound of Mozart melodies and tinkling glasses. With only their heads peeping out from under the duvet, Isadora Elzbeth and Penguin gave a forlorn look around the room. In the soft lamplight everything took on a strange night-time character. The Cinderella wardrobe looked taller and deeper, the telescope looked rounder and fatter. Something glistened on the desk, something fluttered up the chimney. Every now and again Isadora Elzbeth could have sworn she saw something moving from the corner of her eye, but when she turned to look everything stared brazenly back at her, perfectly still.

'Isn't it very unsettling?' she said to Penguin.

Penguin shifted uncomfortably. 'I think there is a spring poking into my back.'

He crawled out from under the duvet and jumped down onto the floor.

'Look at this collection of cheap junk. What a tacky mish-mash of kitsch.'

He dragged a silver slipper out from under the bed and chewed it for a bit. Then he sauntered over to a full-length mirror that leaned against the wall. It had a gilt frame of pears and twisted leaves, and chunks of the gilt fruit had fallen off. Penguin stretched up and began sharpening his nails by dragging them down the length of the frame. A plume of gold and white dust puffed out into the room. Isadora Elzbeth bounded out of bed absolutely horrified.

'Oh God. Don't do that, you're destroying it, you're destroying it!'

Penguin stopped in mid-scratch. 'Please,' he moaned lazily, 'I'm doing it a favour.'

But Isadora Elzbeth wasn't listening. Something was happening in the mirror, her reflection was changing. At first she saw the room and herself and her panic-stricken face all perfectly reflected in the glass. Then she began to change, while the rest of the room stayed perfectly duplicated inside the mirror. Her face became more round. Her hair lightened into long gold twists. Her grey eyes turned peppermint green, her pale lips grew pinker. Her nightdress changed into an old-fashioned blue silk gown and her bare feet grew brown button-up boots. Everything changed, until finally the girl in the mirror was no longer herself.

Isadora Elzbeth was looking at a stranger, a pretty girl with marmalade-coloured hair. The unusual thing was that the girl in the mirror seemed to see her, because she nodded her head ever so slightly and dipped a little curtsey. Confused, Isadora Elzbeth curtseyed back.

'Hello,' she whispered.

The girl in the mirror began to move her mouth, but no sound came. She seemed to be speaking urgently, her peppermint-green eyes had questions in them. At last the girl in the mirror raised her hand. She was pointing at Isadora Elzbeth or to something behind her. Isadora Elzbeth turned around, but there was nothing except the desk loaded down with bric-a-brac. When she turned back, the girl was gone, only her own reflection looked back.

'Who is in the mirror?' Isadora Elzbeth asked herself as she searched every detail in case the strange girl was hiding.

It was Mrs. Buck who found her standing in front of the mirror asking her reflection 'Who is she?'

'What can it mean?' Mrs. Buck asked, having been told of the mystery. She stood behind Isadora Elzbeth and sipped on a round shallow glass that had something clear and bubbly in it. Her crushed-plum lipstick had been freshly applied and her brown, inquisitive eyes had a penetrating dizzy look, as though they were trying to focus on the question she had just asked. Christina was standing by the window looking out at the white moon; she seemed to talk to it more than anybody else in the room.

'It means she's still upset. Her mind is trying to get used to the idea of . . . of . . . never seeing her . . . pare . . .'

Christina didn't bother finishing the sentence.

'But what did you mean?' Mrs. Buck persisted. Then she asked with a secretive expression on her face, 'What exactly did you see in the mirror?'

'I changed in the mirror.' Isadora Elzbeth explained. 'I turned into another girl.'

Christina came towards her. She reached out her hand and began to smooth down Isadora Elzbeth's hair.

'You must feel like someone else, after everything that has happened to you. And perhaps you are not the same person you were before . . . before . . . the accident. It has changed us all, but of course you feel it the hardest.'

Isadora Elzbeth stepped away from Christina. She didn't want to be reminded.

Mrs. Buck collapsed onto the bed and became occupied with the picture painted on the headboard. Penguin tried falling asleep sitting up. Christina went back to examining the moon. Everyone became lost in their own thoughts so Isadora Elzbeth found herself something to be fascinated by. It was on the table among all the other curiosities. It caught her eye because something sparkled inside. How had she not noticed it before? It was a round glass ball, as big as a beach ball, and inside it was a fantastic model of a stormy sea with a galleon that looked as though it was sinking. She picked it up and inspected it more closely. In the soft lamplight the world between her hands glistened. The galleon had a hundred red sails and a mermaid carved on the bow. A small light emanated from one of the portholes, and through this window she could see two ladies in old-fashioned dresses. In the sea there were small brightly-coloured fish. White seabirds were scattered among the dangling stars and in the deceptive lamplight they looked as if they were flying freely.

'I think the sea is made of some form of gelatine.' Christina made Isadora Elzbeth jump. She was close beside her, whispering into her ear.

'Look, it wobbles,' she said, taking the globe and shaking it gently. The slate-blue sea trembled, the ship rose and fell, the light in the window quenched for a moment, hidden by the sea swell.

'Isn't it a charming piece?' Christina said, returning it to its wrought-iron stand. 'I inherited it from an old seafaring uncle of mine. He was a very odd one.' Her blue eyes began sparking up. 'They say he had the second sight. He saw things, things that were, things that might be. People went to him to ask what he could see with his second sight. He once told me he saw Death, and that Death was a gentleman. "A gentleman, Christina, a gent'eman doin' his dutee."' She imitated her uncle's slow, drawling accent.

'He was a mischievous old codger. I used to visit him in his cottage by the sea in my student days. He let me make a studio in one of the bedrooms. He had a great big rusty-coloured moustache, or whiskers as he liked to call them. Boy, he could ham it up, with things like, "Me whiskers are bristlin', the wind will be shiftin' to the nor' east." He could really overdo the wise old superstitious sailor bit. I never for one minute swallowed any of his old guff.

His name was Silas. I'm sure he gave himself that name. "Uncle Silas," I'd say, "I don't believe one word that comes out of that mouth of yours. And you can swear as much as you like on your own life and the lives of all those before you, but you're a downright fibber, an embellisher, and, if you can get away with it, a blatant, flagrant liar!" Here Christina paused. She was standing with her back to the fireplace, her eyes were animated and she smiled.

'Most people would run you from their door if you called them a liar. But Uncle Silas knew he'd been discovered and he enjoyed the fact that I wasn't fooled by him. He had twinkling eyes and in all my years of knowing him I only saw him angry once, but that's another story.' Her eyes glanced away and rested on the green globe with the sea and the ship inside it. 'For years he insisted he had been given the globe by a Russian fisherman named Holgarth, but, on his death bed. . .' She digressed. 'You know, he had a very jolly death. I never saw anyone so fearless and so less like dying in my entire life. He phoned me up one day. "Christina," he said, "I'll be leavin' these parts and wanderin' to the big sea in the sky!" I told him to stop jibbering and to make some sense.

"I'm phoning to tell you I'm dying."

"Of what?" I asked quietly.

"Of too much life," he piped up, "I've lived long enough. All my friends are gone and I don't much care for me own company, so I'm off now. Will you come and see me?"

You wouldn't believe the scene when I got to his

cottage. A congregation of people dressed in black, gliding in and out, lighting candles, saying prayers, whispering and keening over him as if he was laid out stiff and cold in the bed with his heart frozen inside him! I thought, "Oh my God, I'm too late." I ran up the stairs, pushed past the line of women, who had all kissed him at some point – he was a wonderful womaniser. Anyway, I ran past all these broken-hearted women and burst into his bedroom expecting to see his wasted corpse manicured and in repose on his huge brass bed. Instead, there he was, sitting up as bold as you like, sipping tea and dictating his will to the town solicitor! A more healthy, robust man you could not hope to see in your entire life.

"Come in, Christina," he said, "and kiss my rugged handsome face."

"Uncle Silas, I'm disgusted," I said. "You don't look remotely like you're dying!"

This made him laugh. "Girlie," he says, "I'll be gone by mornin'. I've decided to give you the sea." He pointed vigorously at the window, and there on the sill in the blazing light of the morning sat the globe.

"I thought you'd like it, you've admired it so much in the past. I just hope it's not an albatross about yer neck. I think it's charmed meself."

With that he turned to his lawyer and in a dignified, clipped accent that made him sound ridiculous he added, "And in conclusion to the last phrase of the terminal clause, I herewith bequeath my globe to my niece, the painter Christina Seery." The solicitor took it all down, and got my uncle's signature, which revealed his name to be Patrick James Seery.

By the afternoon the house emptied out, except for two women who kept making sandwiches downstairs. The day disappeared in a haze of pipe smoke and stories. Uncle Silas was in fine form. Towards evening, however, I noticed a grey pallor creep over his face. His lips were slowly but perceptibly turning blue. He sank lower into his pillows. He seemed to be shrinking, fading before my very eyes.

"Are you sleepy?" I asked him. "Shall I go?"

"If ye want to, child. But I'd prefer you to see me off."

So I stayed. I thanked him for the Russian globe, and then he told me a story he had never told me before.

"It may not be Russian," he admitted, "it may be Bavarian. It was given to me by my own true love, for my own true love was a Bavarian." He chuckled here. "She were a buxom lass, the way I likes my maids, with a god-awful temper, and such a sharp tongue. She marched everywhere, thump, thump, thump, but I loved her. When I told her the sea was callin' and I better be returnin' home, she flung that globe at me, but I caught it and then I ran. She came thumpin' along the streets after me, hollerin' and bellowin' that I was a 'snake' and a 'spineless slithering rat'. I lost her down one of the side streets in the city. Then I made my way to the ship, the *Oracle*. I ran, because I knew she'd be down after me and I knew that she'd rather shoot me dead than let me go. I don't think I have ever hoisted anchor so quickly in my entire life. We pushed off shore, me and my crew of gallant men – all long dead, God bless them – we pushed off shore and drifted downriver and out to sea, and I saw my true love never more." Then he sighed, "but perhaps I'll see her soon."

He turned his great big hairy face towards me and reached out his hand.

"I am slippin' into the last big voyage."

I remember huffing at him. I told him not to be so poetic. He nodded and smiled. "Aye," he said, "death is very character-buildin'." And with that he died.'

Christina looked about her. Mrs. Buck lay softly snoring on the bed, Isadora Elzbeth was curled up beside her dozing off, her lids slowly closing. Only Penguin was wide awake and enthralled. He sat on the desk beside the globe, staring fixedly into its dark trembling waters.

'I see fish,' he said, then he licked the glass to see if it was sugary.

'Look at that,' Christina said, 'I've bored them to sleep!' Then stroking Penguin's head she whispered, 'Let's you and me have a brandy, to console our poor tired minds.'

Penguin followed her out of the room down to the fire where the embers glowed and Bach played softly on the CD player.

Six

Isadora Elzbeth awoke to the sound of Mrs. Buck calling from the roof.

'Christina, Christina, I think it's on fire. It is, it's definitely on fire. Christina, how do you turn the bloody thing off?'

She could hear all of this quite clearly, because the long window in her room was wide open and the early morning light fell in a yellow slant across the wooden floor. Penguin ran into the room and bounded like a dark streak out of the window. Christina appeared, just as suddenly, carrying a fire extinguisher. She dashed past, said a quick 'good morning' and disappeared along the same route. Above her, Isadora Elzbeth heard the frantic sound of running feet, clanging and thumping.

'Oh for pity's sake, Marian, I told you to watch it.'

'I did watch it. It's uncon-bloody-trollable. What do you mean? I did watch it. I've a headache. I watched it, then the rashers caught fire. The whole damned breakfast is ruined.'

There was a sudden gaseous hiss and then a gushing sound. Christina had turned the fire extinguisher onto the makeshift barbecue. Isadora Elzbeth climbed to the roof just in time to see Christina's extinguisher spewing white foam over an ancient gas burner, some bricks and an old rack that now held the charred remains of the breakfast.

'It was a stupid idea,' Christina muttered to herself. 'I'm going to have to get a new burner if I want to get that balloon up.'

'What's going on, Marian?' Isadora Elzbeth asked.

'It was Christina's idea,' Mrs. Buck said sulkily. 'We came up here this morning and thought we could use the burner from the balloon to cook breakfast on the roof. We assembled a basic barbecue and I almost had my hair burned off.' She sat huffily on one of the garden chairs and looked stonily at her feet. Christina took Penguin on as her ally.

'Penguin, darling, let's leave Mrs. Sulky Boots to calm herself. We'll go to the kitchen and I'll make us all a coffee and throw some croissants into the oven.' With that she descended the narrow steps, her silver hair flowing out behind her, her long gold dressing-gown flapping elegantly around her ankles.

'Well, haven't they just turned into the best of friends,' Mrs. Buck snapped pettishly. Then she fumbled for a cigarette and sat puffing on it angrily.

Isadora Elzbeth sat at the edge of the green pool, where tiny orange fish gleamed in the green water, lily-pads floated over mossy patches and a copper frog looked up at the sky with one hand stretched out to see if it would rain. It was her first time to wake up in Dublin and Isadora Elzbeth felt horribly lonely. The awful strangeness of the place made her feel sore inside.

'Did you sleep well?' Mrs. Buck asked her, her voice sounding slightly croaky.

Isadora Elzbeth looked towards her and blinked away the glare of the blue sky.

'I did, Marian. Did you sleep well?'

'No,' Mrs. Buck sighed, 'I had an infernal dream that kept going round and round in my head. I am sorry about being so cross this morning. I hate it when stupid things happen. I hope I haven't terrified you.' Mrs. Buck leaned forward and looked pleadingly at Isadora Elzbeth.

'Not at all, Marian. I am not afraid of your temper. What was your dream?'

'Oh that.' Mrs. Buck sat back into her chair; she looked a bit stricken this morning. Her hair hadn't been combed and it stood up at the back in a clump. Her eyes looked bleary and small and her skin was a faint greenish colour. She had a crumpled blue cotton nightdress on and over it she wore a long, belted leopardskin coat. She had black boots on her feet that she hadn't bothered to lace up and her hands trembled as she held another cigarette to her lips and fumbled in her pockets for matches.

'My dream, my dream.' Her voice kept roughing up.

Mrs. Buck was definitely hung over and the cigarettes were taking their toll. 'Oh, darling, I have the most splitting headache.' She pulled out a pair of black sunglasses and eased them on. She sighed with relief, lit her cigarette and began to tell her dream.

'It was about some fat, annoying woman, who wanted to travel the seas in search of her one true love. I don't know how I knew her, but I knew her and I had to go with her. She had some kind of hold over me. Boy, was she annoying, with big waspish-red hair. I spent most of the night trying to nudge her out of my head, but she kept coming back. She was very bossy, with a big booming bossy voice. That's probably why I have a headache, her shouting in my head the whole night long. "Do as you are told," she kept screeching, "do as you are told, before I whip you into obedience!" She had a big knobbly face and a thick Teutonic accent. You know, the more I think about it, it was a very vivid dream, sharp and clear, almost like I was there beside her telling her to shut up!'

Here she took a long draw on her cigarette and turned to look at the blush-coloured magnolias flowering down in the neglected garden.

'Here we are!'

Christina's cheery head appeared over the edge of the roof. She climbed up bearing a large tray of steaming croissants and boiling hot coffee. Penguin followed, looking utterly foolish. Christina had tied a napkin around his neck, and it hung so low that it dragged on the ground and tripped him up every few steps.

'I've had a phone call,' Christina said, sitting smugly down and gathering everyone to the table. 'A private buyer wants to look at my collection. He intends to purchase five pieces!'

Mrs. Buck looked amazed. 'Christina, that's wonderful.'

Isadora Elzbeth raised her small, serious face and blinked her grey bewildered eyes.

'I don't care,' she blurted out, 'I hate it here,' and with that she burst into heart-wrenching tears. 'I want to go home,' she wailed, 'please, please, let me go home.' There was a flurry all around her. Christina was hugging her, Mrs. Buck was patting her head from across the table. Penguin had scrambled onto her lap and was nibbling her chin, because it was the only part of her he could reach.

'Shhh, shhh,' Christina whispered, 'it's not so bad here.'

'I don't like it,' Isadora Elzbeth moaned. 'Please let me go home, please, Marian,' she begged. 'I can look after myself, I'm old enough now. Please let me go home.' She sank down onto the table and wept hopelessly into her folded arms. All the while everyone stroked her. Marian petted her hair, Christina rubbed her back and Penguin screwed his head into her chest, affectionately trying to bore his way to her heart. She cried and cried and cried, until she was exhausted, until she had no more tears, until she was limp and raw with grief.

'They're never coming back, are they?'

And Mrs. Buck whispered very softly, 'No, darling. Mammy and daddy are never coming back.'

46

'We could dig them up,' suggested Penguin, 'just to check.'

Christina clipped the back of his head. 'That's a stupid idea.' Isadora Elzbeth wondered how Penguin's meow could possibly have given such offence.

'He was only thanking you for the breakfast,' she said defending him, and taking him in her arms she carried him over to the pond to nibble croissants and feed the fish.

Christina looking at Isadora Elzbeth but speaking to Marian said, 'We have to keep her busy. Why don't you look through my paintings with her this morning, arrange them in the studio for my client this afternoon. I have to go and find a new burner if we want this balloon journey to happen tomorrow night. You can both set your favourite paintings against the wall and if the buyer needs to see any more he can ask me.'

And so it was agreed that Isadora Elzbeth should spend her first morning in Dublin selecting paintings.

Seven

'*He was handsome, no matter what way you look at it.*'
Mrs. Buck stood admiring one of Christina's paintings.
'The Archangel Gabriel,' Mrs. Buck said and Isadora Elzbeth came to look. A man stood in the shadows of some
Gothic ruin. He had dark magnetic eyes that gazed search-
ingly out of the picture. Christina had painted two glass
coloured wings extending in a sweep from his back. He
was beautiful. Mrs. Buck continued rummaging through
the neat stacks of paintings, pulling out her favourite ones
and leaning them against the wall. Every new painting held
a fascination for Isadora Elzbeth. She felt attracted to them
like a moth to light. There were deserted landscapes,
twisted dead trees rising out of evening mists into a twilight sky, there were lost cities, empty and heart-broken.
Mrs. Buck found one that was of a lush garden with

shattered pieces of sculpture lying about. There was a Latin inscription on one of the plinths, *Et in Arcadia ego.*

'What does it mean, Marian?' Isadora Elzbeth asked, leaning over Mrs. Buck's shoulder.

'It means, "Even in Paradise I am", or, to put it more grammatically correct, "I am even in Paradise".' Mrs. Buck shifted uncomfortably in her unlaced boots. She took a puff from the butt end of a French cigarette that she had found in the fireplace and faced the situation by removing her sunglasses and balancing them on top of her head.

Isadora Elzbeth asked the obvious question, 'Who is in Paradise?' She saw Mrs. Buck turn her eyes towards the ceiling as though she wished for divine intervention to take her away from the conversation.

'Death.' The word came like a shower of ashes, in a whisper. 'It means that, even in Paradise, Death must come. Death will have its way. We all must die.'

They both looked into the dull green shadows of the painting and saw the faint traces of afternoon light fall mutely over the grass. The broken statues were once intact, the garden was once neat, this place had at one time been visited by people who were now long dead and gone. Isadora Elzbeth felt her heart pressing against her lungs. She felt lonely for the way the garden once was. She could imagine how beautiful it must have been in its day, all pink roses and trimmed hedges. Mrs. Buck sighed helplessly. 'The bloody Romans. They had a saying for everything. I don't know why Christina has to concentrate on such grim themes. Honestly, I'd swear it's all Gabriel's influence.'

49

But Isadora Elzbeth whispered, 'You don't understand, Marian. They all tell a story.' Isadora Elzbeth had fallen under the spell of the dark, leafy arbours, the moss-covered statues, the wild moorlands and the empty skies where old echoes disappeared. 'They're very atmospheric, Marian.' And Mrs. Buck laughed and stroked the top of Isadora Elzbeth's dark lustrous head. 'I'm glad you like them, but, to be honest, they make me very gloomy. She seems to paint every "death" theme there is. Look at this one of Joan of Arc – she was martyred – and this one, "The Legend of the Wandering Jew", and this one, "The Medieval Dance of Death".'

'Do they all want to die?'

The question stopped Mrs. Buck in her tracks. She looked confused, she flicked her eyes over the paintings and back to Isadora Elzbeth's face.

'My God,' she whispered, 'I never saw that before. Yes, they do. They all want to die.'

'Because they are not afraid,' Isadora Elzbeth said, but Mrs. Buck was dumbstruck and shaking her head, until finally Isadora Elzbeth tapped her on the shoulder and said, 'Why don't you have a shower, Marian? You'll feel fresher and better. Showers always sparkle people up. I can choose the ten paintings, if you like. I don't mind, I like the paintings. They're spooky.'

Mrs. Buck laughed, a tinkling, refreshing laugh that made Isadora Elzbeth think of forget-me-nots.

'A shower is an excellent idea. See you in a bit.' And she left.

While Penguin snoozed on the windowsill, with one paw dangling, and Mrs. Buck showered with lemon-scented soap, Isadora Elzbeth chose ten of her favourite paintings. When she had finished, she sat down on the window ledge and looked out at the maze of streets below her. The people looked like specks weaving around each other. Isadora Elzbeth's mind blurred looking at them. She dreamed of the pear tree at the end of her garden at home. She dreamed of the river and the long wavy grasses and the rushes that swayed in the breeze. And just as she was about to remember her mother's voice, Penguin's rough tongue licked her eye and brought her back to the present.

'Where did they go?' Isadora Elzbeth asked, 'and what shall we do without them?' Before Penguin could answer, a newly scrubbed and fabulously attired Mrs. Buck walked through the door.

'I thought we'd go to the Shelbourne for lunch. All three of us,' she chirped. 'I have been dreaming of their scones and clotted cream and thick Kenyan coffee for ages now.' The shower had lifted Mrs. Buck's spirits. Her face was glowing. 'Besides,' she went on, 'it's time you walked around Dublin and stopped looking at it from a bird's-eye view. Well, come along, get dressed. Let's go.'

By twelve-thirty everyone was smartly groomed and ready. They marched down the gloomy staircase, with its worm-eaten banisters and rickety steps. Mrs. Buck had to kick the front door before turning the latch. 'It's the only way to open it,' she explained, half-laughing at the absurdity. When she did open the door a swell of noise and sunshine burst through.

The loud rattle of car engines, the screech of buses, the chatter of people talking, the squeak of bicycle brakes, the metal slam of van doors opening and closing delivering goods. The swirling distraction of it all made Isadora Elzbeth a little shy. She reached for Mrs. Buck's hand and felt more secure when Mrs. Buck's soft fingers lightly squeezed hers and she guided her out across the road.

'Morning, Christy,' Mrs. Buck called in to the butcher, who waved back at her.

'This way,' she told Penguin, who, for some reason, had become fascinated by a rogue Brussels sprout that had rolled off a vegetable stall right under his nose.

It was a beautiful day and everyone seemed cheery. A fresh breeze cooled the boiling sun, making the temperature very pleasant. Strangers smiled and greeted strangers and Isadora Elzbeth noticed how there seemed to be room enough for everyone. As they wound through the streets past red-bricked Victorian buildings, homing pigeons swooped, and Mrs. Buck told the story of how greedy pigeons can eat until they explode into a gaseous pile of guts and feathers. Penguin was very amused. He laughed heartily.

As they made their way through St. Stephen's Green they climbed over a humped-back bridge and saw tiny fluffy ducklings. Isadora Elzbeth counted seven of them. 'They're so small they could fit into the palm of my hand,' she announced, and they all giggled as the ducklings paddled frantically, bumping into each other, their compact downy bodies spinning forward in circles and at tangents. The green water of the pond darkened into pools of brown beneath the shady trees, and Isadora Elzbeth whispered what no one else could hear, '*Et in Arcadia ego.*'

The Shelbourne Hotel had red-carpeted steps. It was the first time Isadora Elzbeth had been through a swing-door. She went round twice, not sure when to jump out, and then she had to go in again to free Penguin from the circular trap.

Mrs. Buck was already in the tea room. 'Isn't this pleasant,' she said, looking around the elegant room with its grand piano and polished clocks. She liked the flimsy eighteenth-century wall paintings and the ornate baroque vases that were scattered among the veneered furniture. Isadora Elzbeth felt as if she was in a library and thought it best to whisper if she had to speak.

A lady came over and asked them if they would like to see the menu. Penguin said, 'Thank you, Ma'am, that would be delightful,' but Mrs. Buck ignored him and requested coffee and scones all round. Everything was brought out with such ceremony. The silver coffee-pot was placed on a tiny three-legged stand, the scones were piled onto the napkin-lined plate, the clotted cream and jam came in delicate white dishes. Mrs. Buck sighed with deep satisfaction at the ware spread before her. They began eating. A manageress came forward to complain about 'the cat', but Mrs. Buck took her aside and spoke to her, which seemed to solve the situation. She returned to her big soft chair and winked victoriously at Penguin. Then her eyes suddenly flung wide with astonishment as she looked beyond Penguin towards a tall man who was approaching their table.

'Marian. I thought it was you.' The man extended his large hand and leaned jovially towards Mrs. Buck, kissing both her cheeks.

'And how gorgeous you look, unusual as ever.'

Mrs. Buck laughed coquettishly. 'Johannes, how come that sounds vaguely insulting?'

'Nonsense, you're one of the most stylish women in Dublin. With such charming accessories.' His hawk-green eyes glanced brightly around the table. 'Aren't you going to introduce us?'

Mrs. Buck purred with amusement. 'Isadora Elzbeth, I'd like to introduce you to Johannes Handley, and this is Penguin.' Johannes bowed deeply.

So this was the artist whose opening they were going to fly to in a scarlet balloon. He was a distinguished-looking man with aquiline features, a thin pointed nose and ruddy cheeks. His jaw was sharp, his eyes were sharp, his wit was sharp. While Isadora Elzbeth looked at him, he entertained Mrs. Buck and Penguin with his merry good humour. His solid, tall body, dressed completely in black, dominated the room. He wore chunky silver rings on each of his fingers and moved his hands in big broad gestures to punctuate what he was saying. He was telling some story about being stopped by the police while cycling home without a light at two o'clock in the morning.

'Which is all well and good,' he said. 'I thanked them

for their observation and promised them I'd buy a new light. I was in such a hurry to get away, I cycled into an open drain. I felt a right fool crawling up out of it, with the police laughing and saying, "If ye'd a light sir, ye'd know where ye were going!" Well, I'd best be off. You'll be there tomorrow night?'

Mrs. Buck looked momentarily ashamed, a guilty flush swept across her cheeks.

'Yes,' she answered, afraid to look at Isadora Elzbeth. 'Yes, em, thank you. Everything prepared?'

Johannes rolled his green eyes to heaven. 'The headache,' he moaned, pressing his hand in mock-theatrical fashion to his forehead.

'Everything in the catalogue was printed either back-wards or upside down. I thought I'd never get Stranvinskiney to agree to open it, and then yesterday I heard that the security staff may go on strike!' Mrs. Buck seemed genuinely shocked by the prospect of a strike. 'If that happens I will emigrate. I swear to you, Marian, the heartache, you know how tedious the creative process is, fleshing an idea out, constructing its meaning . . .'

Even Penguin began to doze off. Mrs. Buck thought it best to interrupt.

'Yes, the agony of art. But it shall all bear fruit. I heard a rumour,' she paused here and looked significantly around the room. 'I heard that the museum has purchased one of your pieces.'

Johannes smiled broadly, confirming that the rumour was in fact quite true.

'Now, Marian,' he said coyly, 'you mustn't believe everything you hear.'

He looked towards the door and informed them all that he had to go and organise the wine.

'Can you believe, the guest list was over a thousand people this time?' His horror was not authentic; Johannes was proud to have so many people to ask and he couldn't help boasting about it.

He was about to leave when he enquired, almost as an afterthought. 'So how is the delicious Christina? Beaten anyone up lately?' He playfully touched his right eye, and smiled sardonically at an old memory.

Mrs. Buck laughed at him. 'Only those who step out of line,' she said, for she knew he had never taken the punch-up seriously.

'Good for her!' Johannes kissed Mrs. Buck's hand and bowed his goodbyes to Isadora Elzbeth and Penguin.

'I hope she'll be there tomorrow night,' he called back as he stepped through the door.

'Oh she'll be there all right,' Mrs. Buck informed him, then, turning conspiratorially towards the table, she repeated, 'she'll be there.'

Isadora Elzbeth couldn't understand it. She liked Johannes Handley, so why did Christina and Mrs. Buck want to spoil his big night? She finished her scone, every now and again glancing disapprovingly at Mrs. Buck. It was while they were walking home through the park that she finally plucked up the courage to ask, 'Why do you and Christina not like Johannes Handley?'

Mrs. Buck was sincerely astounded. 'Of course we like him. We were in college together, we were great friends, still are. This thing tomorrow night, it's just a humorous stunt. To be honest, they're very competitive, Christina and Johannes. It'll all be a bit of a laugh, good fun arriving in such style to an opening, in a red balloon. Honestly, it will be such good fun.'

Isadora Elzbeth was not sure. Having reached 30 Wexford Street they pushed open the black door, filed up the dreary staircase and into the flat, only to find Christina surrounded by unopened parcels and sipping tea in the company of an oriental man.

Eight

'Hello!' Christina sprang to her feet. 'This is Mr. Sim.'

Mr. Sim slid up to a standing position and, interlocking his fingers before his chest, he bowed with a slight tip of his head. He had beetle-black hair, fine small bones, watchful eyes and a mobile phone bulging from the top pocket of his immaculate dark-blue suit.

'He works for the Tushian Corporation. They would like to buy my paintings to give as gifts to their most regular clients,' Christina explained. She looked meaningfully at Mrs. Buck, and Isadora Elzbeth wondered what was going on.

'Mr. Sim prefers post neo-modernism himself, but his boss likes my stuff.'

'I am quite in agreement with you, Mr. Sim. However, I am Christina's agent, and I should tell you that, despite the fact that her work is anachronistic, it does possess a certain post-modern edge. Shall we go into the studio?'

In the space of one sentence Mrs. Buck had turned into an efficient businesswoman whose descriptions of Christina's paintings left Isadora Elzbeth confused. What did post-modernism mean? Did it have anything to do with the modern postal system?

'Watch her,' Christina whispered to Isadora Elzbeth, 'she's poetry in motion.'

'We've narrowed the selection down, but of course should you wish to see more . . .' Mr. Sim nodded in response to Mrs. Buck's information.

They slowly examined each work, Mrs. Buck speaking occasionally. Mr. Sim lingered over each of the canvases. He produced a magnifying glass from his pocket and scrutinised each painting as though he were checking a microchip for a fatal flaw. Everything was going along fine, until Mrs. Buck stood over the portrait of an aristocratic elderly lady which Isadora Elzbeth had found right at the back of the piles of paintings.

'Who is this?' Mr. Sim asked disparagingly.

But Mrs. Buck couldn't answer. Her eyes blinked with disbelief. She was trying to repress some kind of horror, when Christina stepped forward and laughed merrily.

'Oh, Marian, you know this is not one of mine.' She took the portrait up and looked at it warmly. 'It's such a quirky painting, isn't it? I bought a trunk at an auction and this portrait was inside. What a grand dame she is. She looks so formidable, I don't think I'd like to cross her. Her name is written on the cuff of her sleeve.' Christina read it aloud, 'Blythe Castiglione.' Mrs. Buck almost choked, on hearing the name. She faked a cough and excused herself to gulp down a glass of water. Isadora Elzbeth ran after her, afraid that somehow she might have ruined the whole deal.

'Oh, Marian,' Isadora Elzbeth pleaded, leaning into the sink to confess all, 'I am so sorry, I thought Christina had painted it, and I liked the painting of the fat woman, so I chose it. I hope it doesn't make Mr. Sim go away, I hope he buys something, I hope I haven't ruined everything.' Isadora Elzbeth's voice was disappearing down the plug hole like a slow trickle of water. Mrs. Buck put down the glass and looked pensively around her.

'Oh nonsense,' she whined, trying desperately to sound jolly. 'It's my own foolishness child, it has nothing to do with you. I got a little fright, that's all. You see, Blythe Castiglione is the woman who kept shouting at me in my dreams last night.' Even Isadora Elzbeth was surprised. 'The thing is,' Mrs. Buck continued, 'I'd swear blind in a court of law that I had never seen that portrait of her before now. So how did she turn up in my dreams last night?' Mrs. Buck shivered at the eerie thought that perhaps somehow she might be psychic.

Then her chocolate-brown eyes smoothed over. 'This is nonsense,' she told herself, 'it's just one of those weird things that happens.' She brightened up, smacked her lips with resolution and said, 'Come on, we can't afford to let the heebie-jeebies lose us the Tushian deal.' She squared her shoulders and returned to Mr. Sim, who was speaking enthusiastically to Christina about her work. Isadora Elzbeth did not follow her.

Penguin found Isadora Elzbeth on the roof. She was sitting by the pool, looking glumly into the greeny water.

'Hey, sunshine!' he meowed, 'big deals going on down there, but what of it, when can a cat get some sardines around here?'

'There's nothing wrong,' Isadora Elzbeth replied, completely misunderstanding Penguin. 'I needed some time to think.' She leaned over and stroked Penguin's head. 'I think it's very odd here. Strange things keep happening, like the girl in the mirror and now the woman in the painting, and I can't help thinking about what the crow said when he flew back and almost bit my nose off. He said there was *a globe an apple and a star that is a snake, Isadora Elzbeth go in search of death.* But I don't know what that means.' She looked sadly at the basket and the scarlet sailcloth that fluttered loosely around it. 'I'm not too sure I want to fly in that thing,' she confided. 'I wish everything had just stayed the way it was.' Penguin played with the ends of her hair. 'I wish nothing had changed.' She was on the verge of tears when Mrs. Buck's head popped up over the edge of the roof.

'Mr. Sim's gone. And guess what, it looks like he'll take more than ten paintings!'

Christina's voice came from somewhere below. 'Everybody come on. I have a surprise.'

'I hope it's a champagne surprise,' Mrs. Buck chirrupped as she descended. When Isadora Elzbeth and

Penguin joined the others in the living-room they were drinking champagne, laughing and talking loudly while the Rolling Stones were blaring from the CD player.

'The surprise,' Christina shouted, falling to her knees and spreading the parcels piled on the floor. She encouraged everyone to open one. The wrapping paper crinkled out in strips and shreds around them. Penguin dived around, delighted to make a nuisance of himself.

Swathes of ornate material spilled out onto the floor. Intricate patterns of pearl and diamanté beading appeared formlessly among the jumbled pile. Christina pulled two corners up to her shoulders and stood making perfect sense of the purple striped silk and white lace edges.

'See, it's a dress. A baroque costume. Imagine, ladies once had to wear dresses like this every day!'

The dress was a construction. A bone bodice tapered into a slender waist, and the skirt was draped over a whale-bone cage that exaggerated the hips, standing out at right angles, making it impossible to walk through any door without having to dip sideways first. The neckline plunged low, and the tight-fitting sleeves were trimmed with layers of moth-eaten lace. Mrs. Buck held up her dress; it was orange and in the same style.

'And this is Isadora Elzbeth's.' Christina pulled up a miniature version of the other dresses, the only difference being that Isadora Elzbeth's dress was green and printed on the wide skirt was a map of the world. It looked just the right size, and poking from underneath the shreds of brown paper she saw two small glass slippers.

'They're your shoes. Aren't they gorgeous? Look at the beading.'

'Explain all of this to me.' Mrs. Buck was leaning on the sofa, her elbow compressing the leather cushion.

'Simple,' Christina said, her round face lit by the eagerness in her blue eyes.

'When we go to the show tomorrow night, in the balloon, we will wear these costumes. For the fun of it. We will look so stylish. And, anyway, it's kind of appropriate. I mean historically. These costumes were worn in Bavaria in the 1760s when the first air balloon was invented. Of course, the history books don't see it that way. They think the first hot-air balloon was invented in 1783 by the two Montgolfier brothers, but I have it on good authority that the first hot-air balloon was invented by a woman, in Bavaria, in the 1760s.'

Penguin shook his head. 'Hot air is right! Women know all about it, talking hot air. I believe you when you say a woman invented the hot-air balloon.'

Christina ignored him. 'This same woman might have also discovered the recipe for porcelain.'

'Now I know you're lying,' Penguin snorted, 'Everybody knows you don't cook porcelain. See, hot air!'

Isadora Elzbeth took Penguin down off the mantelpiece. 'He's a little anxious about heights. I think he's worried about tomorrow's flight.' She carried him out to the kitchen and fed him ice-cream mixed with sardines.

Nine

That night Isadora Elzbeth couldn't sleep. She felt uneasy.

'I feel like I have changed for ever, that I will never be the same again, since. . .' but she couldn't say 'since the accident', so she just said 'since' and left Penguin to guess the rest. 'Do you think you've changed?'

Penguin shoved his nose under the pillow and shut his eyes.

'No, I don't suppose cats think about things like that. It's just that I was thinking about engines the other day. A car is a machine and its engine is its heart, pumping petrol around its tubes and things and making it work. To stop it, you turn off the key in the ignition.' Isadora Elzbeth became completely engrossed in this conversation with herself. She sat upright in her bed and spoke earnestly to her own shadow, which was reflected by the lamp onto the wall.

'Then, you see, I thought about my heart beating. Ba boom, ba boom, ba boom. My heart is an engine and death is the key that turns it off. But do I step out of the car? That is the question?'

Isadora Elzbeth's shadow nodded from the opposing wall. 'Where do I go when I die? Where did Mammy and Daddy go?' This was too horrible a question to ponder, so she moved along to her next question. 'Everyone thinks that they are what they see in the mirror. But I was thinking, you can't see your own voice and nobody knows where thoughts begin. Do they start inside or outside your head? So, if you can't see your thoughts and your voice is invisible, how can you be sure you've thought what you said?'

Isadora Elzbeth's line of argument became confused, and her eyebrows puckered as she tried to smooth out her ideas.

'Let me explain shadow.' Penguin buried his head deeper beneath his pillow and tried desperately to blot out the sound of Isadora Elzbeth's chatter. 'Engines are important, they are inside things. You are my shadow, you do not exist without me. My heart is my engine, I do not exist without it. That must mean that everything has an engine. The moon has an engine because the light is always on and something keeps turning it about in the sky. But I'm not too sure if a stone has an engine.'

At this point the fizzle went out of Isadora Elzbeth's

conversation, even her shadow seemed disinterested. She gazed about the room and the room gazed back at her. For a while she sang a doleful tune about moths, making up the words as she went along, but after fifteen verses even she got tired of the song. It was while she was idly stroking the blue velvet canopy that hung from the bedpost that she noticed among the books piled against the wall a small leather-bound volume that had no writing on the spine. She slipped out of bed and fetched it. When she flicked through it she realised it wasn't a book, but some kind of diary, filled to the brim with old-fashioned handwriting and squiggly diagrams. She climbed back into bed, fluffed up her pillow, opened the first page and read.

Journal Number X AD 1765
Further accounts documented by the Chemyst
A.S. Wish.

Marianne is so serious she has been reading Greek philosophy, Heraclitus of Ephesus to be exact. She came out into the garden yesterday. I was cutting a box hedge into the shape of a Salamander and I had just got to its winged back, when Marianne broke my concentration by asking me if I believed in reincarnation! She looked at me so seriously that I laughed. She's hardly past her twelfth birthday and she's trying to solve the riddles of the universe. She wouldn't let me escape, I had to answer her. I asked her what she meant. She opened the book she had been reading and very solemnly read aloud

'The soul will be now living now dead.'

Then she asked me to explain what Heraclitus meant.

'Explain it, Sia, how can the soul be now living and now dead? Isn't it either one thing or the other. It can't be the two things at the same time, can it? The soul can't be alive and dead at the same time, or dead and alive at the same time, can it, Sia?'

There she stood in the garden with her green eyes fixing me to the spot. I would have to answer her. Then her question suddenly put me in mind of an experiment I carried out when I was about the same age as she is now. I put my shears onto my unfinished hedge and we walked down to the river.

'Come here,' I said to her. We sat down on a rock and I told her to be quiet for a minute, that I was going to answer her question but first I had to catch a frog. Suddenly Marianne snapped at the grass and brought a little frog up in her cupped hands.

'Now will you answer my question?' she asked.

'My interest in science started when I was your age,' I explained. 'I was down by this river and I saw a frog, and he spoke to me.'

'Sia!' Marianne moaned, 'no fairy stories.'

'He spoke to me in a scientific way. There he was jumping around on his hind legs and I watched him and I watched him, until his limbs became strange things to me, so fascinating that I wanted to examine them closer and see how they worked. That was when I carried out my first dissection.'

'You killed him!'

Poor Marianne, she was horrified and disgusted, and curious at the same time.

'Not only did I kill him,' I went on, 'but in my laboratory I cut him open.'

She didn't want to hear any more details. She wanted to

know what the point to my story was and how was I answering her question about some things being 'now living, now dead'.

'I attached copper wire to the dead frog, dipped the wire in zinc, and the frog jumped.'

Marianne wanted to know how.

'It was charged with energy,' I explained. 'It was dead, but it moved. It is a bit of a crude illustration to my answer. My answer to your question is, things can look alive and be dead at the same time, like my little galvanised frog. As a chemyst I see materials transform when I pour chemycals over them, and chemycals can change from one thing into another. Transformation is at the basis of every chemycal experiment. Who knows what energies are in our bodies? Who knows the chemystry of the soul?'

Marianne looked worried. I couldn't help smiling. 'It reminds me,' I said, 'of something an English playwright once wrote. That there are more things on heaven and earth, Horatio, than are dreamt of in your philosophy.' Marianne turned to me with her sombre little face. 'But,' she whispered, 'that is not all that Heraclitus of Ephesus said.' She placed the frog back into the grass. 'He said the living and the dead are always changing places.'

'What, round and round, swapping places with each other?'

I gave her a cuddle and told her not to be worrying so much about life and the afterlife, that Heraclitus was only writing and that not everything written is worth paying attention to. And anyway, perhaps the true meaning to his text might have been lost in translation. She would have kept on at me, except that Will interrupted.

I hate to see my face in the mirror and think of Will at the same time. I am a monster. How can Marianne be my little sister? She is so pretty, her pale buttery skin, her mint eyes and

barley-gold hair, even her petiteness, all so different to me.
AmbroSia Wish, large, awkward, chunky, I have a slab face and
my hands are too big. I don't see why I had to grow to be almost
six foot tall, taller than any man in the kingdom, except for Will,
who is the same height as me and has the privilege of looking
directly into my murky-coloured eyes whenever we speak. His eyes
have the dark-green sharpness of a hawk, they are the green of
shadows on a river, the green of medicine in a jar, my Will, I
Will . . . not let myself do this.

I will find the Arcanum

There followed pages and pages of symbols added and
subtracted from each other. There were recipes, called
Alchemical recipes, which were so funny that she read
some of them aloud to Penguin. But Penguin didn't seem
interested, so Isadora Elzbeth flicked on to find another
section of writing.

Word has come to us that there is a contagion in the city. We are
not sure how serious it is, but my father has been called away.
Marianne says she wants to be an Alchemist too, except she says
she wants to find the 'philosopher's stone' and make us all immor-
tal so the contagion can't harm us. Will told us a story, that in
Saxony, King Augustus the Second has imprisoned a young man
by the name of John Böttger in his palace. This John Böttger
boasted that he could turn base metal into gold, and more, he
claims to be able to manufacture porcelain. Augustus has taken
him at his word and has him caged up in a room, burning sul-
phur and quicksilver, trying to make tin and nickel into precious

metals. I would be interested in his porcelain experiments though . . . Marianne says that she has noticed a stranger circling our house in the dead of night. She says he is tall, with deep eyes. She caught him looking in the window at her. I am worried. Will has decided to stay now that father is away, to protect us. He is painting Marianne's portrait.

More mathematics, symbols, recipes and little notes, one of which said:

The ware exploded in the firing.

Father has written to us, he says the contagion is devastating, already one-third of the population has been decimated. He thinks it may be a strain of Anthrax. Patients vomit blood, black buboes appear under the armpits and around the groin. The fearful thing is, once contracted, the victim is dead within two days. He thinks the contagion is airborne but there is the possibility that it may be carried in the water. A rash of moths has infested the city, they swarm in dark clouds and sometimes there are so many that they blot out the sun. He says terror has made people mad, reckless, even criminal. He warns us to stay and under no circumstance to come to the city. I feel I should go and help him, but Marianne insists if I go, she goes. She says she is busy working on a cure. She can always make myself and Will laugh. I think I may have to help my father, he cannot be expected to attend to so many sick at his age. Besides, when he set off with Dr. Polidori it was as a consultant, a retired physician sharing his expertise. Things have obviously turned black. I worry for his safety.

My father is dead. We have travelled to the city to give him a proper burial. We have been told that he has been buried in a communal grave. The city is a smoky rathole of infested shadows. People have imprisoned themselves inside their houses, casting their dead loved ones out onto the doorsteps for the 'bogey men' to pick up in their carts and dump them in the pit. The straying few that do roam the streets are half starved, half mad with grief and terror. They run at us screaming, with sunken faces and bulging eyes, begging us to release them from their agony, or haranguing us, or being disturbingly merry, dancing madly to their own cracked tunes. I dragged Marianne away. Will would not let us look for our father. He insists we leave straight away. But I must do something. I have told him that I will stay. He will take Marianne back home.

Four weeks and I must have buried over one thousand people. They drop before me like flies, sores suppurating, vomiting, racked in agony, too weak to speak. I work with a team of two doctors. I am no expert, I do not have my father's knowledge. The hospital is overcrowded, patients spill out into the courtyard and stables. I cannot describe the stench, the air is thick and rancid.

A minute to myself. Marianne's letter and parcel make me smile. She says Will's portrait of her is finished and she thinks he has made her too pretty. She says she caught the man with dark eyes following her. What does he want? I have written to Will to find out who he is and to tell him to get rid of him. She also sends me a jar filled with green liquid. She insists it is the 'cure' she has been working on. She tells me to mix a small tincture and is very

exact about my measures! She swears she has distilled it from the
purest of substances and that she used a fire so hot it burned white
and spat out salamanders. I poured the measure of her recom-
mendation. It smelled of apples and, so help me, I think she has
brewed a delicious liqueur. We could sell it and make a fortune.

Isadora Elzbeth felt thirsty. She nudged Penguin. 'This
is interesting,' she said, 'a bit like a story.' She turned the
page to continue reading, but there was only one sentence,
the rest of the book was all formulas, obviously added at a
much later date. The final sentence read:

Marianne is dead.

'How?' Isadora Elzbeth blinked at the suddenness of it
all. 'But only a minute ago she was burning things and
making green liqueur. How did she die? Who was the man
with dark eyes? Why was he following her? Did he murder her?'

She looked down at Penguin, with his head shoved
under his pillow, and snuggled down beside him to talk to
him. 'It's very sad, Penguin. There was a little girl called
Marianne who caught a frog and made salamanders jump
out of a fire. She had a sister called Sia who was in love with
a painter called Will and one day she looked out of her bedroom window and saw a strange man staring in at her.'

Penguin sucked his head out from under his pillow and
moaned.

'I don't care. Shhh! Sleep now, sleep. Bedtime, shut-
eye time, see.' He slapped a paw gently onto Isadora
Elzbeth's eye.

Her open eye blinked. 'I won't cry, Penguin, but the little girl died and I can't help wondering what happened to the others, to Sia and Will and the dark man prowling about.'

Penguin moved the soft pad of his paw down over her mouth. 'Hush now, banana head, that's enough prattling for one evening. Shush now.'

Ten

Isadora Elzbeth woke up bright as a polished button. A shaft of blond sunlight beamed through the split in the curtains. Penguin was looking at the green globe on the table and singing an old swing tune from the thirties.

'Oh, so you decided to wake up?' He turned his cat face towards her. 'I'm glad you slept so well. How did I sleep, eh? Terrible, that's how. You spent the whole night long running after someone called Marianne, telling her you had to find *the Arcanum*. I could have happily stuffed that stupid journal . . .'

It was a mystery, but for now he understood her perfectly. Isadora Elzbeth rolled out of bed and plonked a fat kiss on top of Penguin's head.

'You're very talkative this morning. Are you nervous? Don't you want to fly in the balloon?'

'Of course I do, I want to bounce around the sky with two mad women who'll probably get drunk and crash us into some transmitter. I can see the headlines now: TWO MAD WOMEN, A YOUNG GIRL AND HER CAT IN BURST BALLOON INCIDENT. It'll be a nasty, shoddy end, us dangling from an aerial, disrupting television transmission. I can't think of a better way to spend an afternoon, except maybe shoving my head into a bucket of water. That might be just a little more fun.'

'The sea is jelly.' Isadora Elzbeth pointed into the globe, overriding Penguin's conversation.

'The ship is an old galleon. I think it is beautiful, it must have one hundred sails. Can you imagine being on something like that? Imagine if we were small enough to fit inside that glass world, sailing on an endless sea, with two fancy ladies, on adventures. You see, you can see the ladies through the porthole.'

Penguin peered into the gelatine sea, an iridescent fish darted beneath the ship's hull.

'Damned fascinating,' he agreed sarcastically. He twitched his ears. 'There is something I must tell you,' he said.

'You're right about this place,' Isadora Elzbeth nodded. 'There is something very weird about here. Too many strange things, the girl in the mirror, and that woman that Marian dreamed about, Blythe Castiglione. The noises in this room at night. The way Christina and Marian don't seem like anybody else I know. Do you think it has something to do with the building. Is 30 Wexford Street haunted? You should know. Cats are more sensitive to apparitions and spooky things.'

Penguin nuzzled through her hair and found her ear. 'I'm starving,' he wailed. 'Hunger, lack of sleep. My mood is black, feed me, feed me.'

'Meow, to you too,' Isadora Elzbeth replied. She took a look at the globe before shrugging her shoulders and putting everything out of her mind, something she was rather good at lately. When Mrs. Buck found her she was holding onto the balcony with her eyes closed, sniffing the air like a Baskerville hound.

'Do you smell trouble?' Mrs. Buck asked.

'I was smelling the lilac,' Isadora Elzbeth explained, 'and listening to the church bells.'

The bells of St. Xavier church pealed out over the glistening rooftops and the peppery fragrance of witch-hazel drifted up out of the neglected garden.

'Breakfast.' Mrs. Buck looked down at the tray she was carrying. 'Strawberries and cream. Sinful I know, but we all need to indulge once in a while.' She winked.

Penguin sauntered out onto the balcony and peered inquisitively over the side.

'Long way down,' he muttered to himself, 'long way down. The fall won't kill me, it's the sudden stop at the end that does it.' He began swaying crazily, round and round, and would have slumped forward and teetered off the edge if Isadora Elzbeth hadn't wrapped her arms around him and told him she was going to try an experiment.

'Co-operate now. I want you to drape across my shoulders like a fur collar.'

She slid Penguin over her head and held onto his front and back paws. 'This is a cool way to carry a cat. Can you do it?'

'No I bloody can't,' Penguin howled. But Isadora Elzbeth thought this was a good sign and she began climbing to the roof.

Marian was pouring coffee when Isadora Elzbeth arrived. She looked up and laughed heartily, her tinkly forget-me-not laugh.

'That's the best way to carry a cat I've ever seen,' she said.

'Shut up, woman! ' Penguin snarled.

Mrs. Buck tweaked his ear. 'You should wear him to the opening just like this! It's very charming!'

Penguin went into a sulk. He skidded down onto his chair and ignored everybody, even Christina, who swooped up onto the roof in her gold nightgown wearing a tiara she'd found in some junk-shop. He refused to snap a sarcastic comment, even though something should have been said. Christina was in her usual bubbly morning mood. Mrs. Buck on the other hand was slow to wake up to the world. She didn't have a hangover this morning, but she still said very little.

Christina chirped on, dragging conversation from Mrs. Buck. Isadora Elzbeth listened in sometimes, but mostly she sank back into her chair and let the sunshine pour all over her. The strawberries were delicious in the warm morning sun. Their taste mingled with the honeyed smells from the neglected garden.

'I suppose it could be classified as a tenement,' Christina was saying. 'I can imagine lots of snotty-nosed kids playing on the stairs. I do know there was a family reared in my place in the forties sometime. Seven kids. God knows where they all slept. And upstairs was a tailor's in the thirties. But before that, at the turn of the century, who knows what 30 Wexford street was. I did hear some vague story of a woman who had supposedly murdered her lover in a passionate rage.'

Isadora Elzbeth suddenly tuned in to the conversation. A flash of Gabriel passed before her eyes. He had disappeared off the face of the earth; supposing Christina had murdered him in some fit? She examined Christina with a suspicious glare, until Mrs. Buck asked, 'What are you scowling at, Isadora Elzbeth?'

'Oh it was only a story,' Christina rattled on. 'I'm sure you're not lying in a murdered man's bed.'

Isadora Elzbeth faked a smile while the women continued talking.

'I do remember Christy telling me about some psychic living here. It must have been in Victorian times, because he said it was a time when everyone went to seances. They were mad about seances in Victorian times, ectoplasm spouting out of everyone's mouth. He said this woman was quite famous, she made the newspapers. I think there may even be a photograph of her with ectoplasm flowing out of her ears.'

'What's ectoplasm?' Isadora Elzbeth asked. Christina shrugged her shoulders, 'it looks like white froth in the photographs. It's white stuff that mediums throw up when they are in a trance, some kind of energy-spouting stuff. The point is that all the photographs are doctored. Nobody has ever spouted ectoplasm, it was just a big Victorian scam to get people to come along to seances. It was a fashionable evening out back then. I don't see why, I'm not so sure I'd want to talk to the dead myself.'

The last remark fell with a heavy thud towards Isadora Elzbeth. She'd have liked very much to talk to her parents. She sat with her eyes sensitively wide thinking about what Christina had just said.

'Nice one!' Penguin couldn't help but get his spoke in. 'Anything else you'd like to say to upset the child?'

Christina flapped into another conversation. 'There were lots of bogus sciences in the past. Science is funny.' She laughed a hollow laugh and tried to generate a bit of interest in what she was saying. 'For years they thought the earth was flat. Ptolomy. Wasn't he Egyptian?' No one was really listening, so Christina rattled on. 'He thought the earth was flat and the centre of the universe. You could sail off the edge of the earth in the thirteenth century. And there were monsters beyond the Rock of Gibraltar, enormous sea beasts with jaws large enough to swallow a ship. It's only since the 1800s that science has become scientific. Before that you had every kind of experiment mixed with magic nonsense. Alchemy. I mean, Newton the father of modern science! He was an alchemist.'

Isadora Elzbeth shot forward in her chair, her catapulting interest made Christina jump back and squeak, 'Oh, I didn't think anyone was listening.'

But Isadora Elzbeth was riveted. 'I was reading about that last night,' she whispered with disbelief.

'Really?' Christina's eyes brightened. 'He was a pig, you know, Newton that is. Tried to set his mother's house on fire when she married a second time. And he wasn't particularly bright at school, so don't worry if your school work is average. Newton was very average until he transformed the world with modern mathematics. I think he invented calculus, but some other guy beat him to the post getting published first.'

She would have drifted on, giving interesting biographical details about Newton if Isadora Elzbeth hadn't pulled her back on track.

'No,' she said raising her small hands dramatically in front of her.

'That's right,' Penguin interrupted, 'tell her to stop.'

'No,' Isadora Elzbeth repeated, 'no no. I was reading about alchemy.'

'Oh, not Newton then.' Christina seemed a tad disappointed. 'So where were you reading about alchemy?'

'In the journal downstairs.'

Christina looked back blankly. It meant nothing to her.

'Have I subscribed to a scientific journal I don't know about?' she asked Mrs. Buck.

'It's not a magazine,' Isadora Elzbeth explained, 'it's like a diary, it's full of handwriting. By this chemist Ambrosia

Wish. She's filled the journal with experiments, but she has written some bits like a diary.'

Christina was interested. 'Where did I get it? What does the book look like?'

'It's red, with no writing on the cover, and it's dated 1765.'

'That's fascinating.' Christina's head was busy trying to figure out how she had the journal, while at the same time being distracted by what Isadora Elzbeth was saying.

'Ambrosia Wish was a chemist. She had a little sister and the plague came to this city and their father was a doctor so he went to help the people who caught the plague, only he died and Marianne was working on being an alchemist. Is an alchemist an old-fashioned chemist?'

Christina looked confused at the question. 'Who is Marianne?' she finally asked.

'Oh that's Sia's – Ambrosia's – little sister. She eventually died, after she'd invented a green liqueur.'

Christina and Mrs. Buck laughed. They had lost the thread of the conversation and were becoming more and more confused.

'I must read it,' Christina admitted, then she exclaimed, 'Revelation! Of course, I got it in the same lot as that portrait of the Countess of Castiglione. I bought this trunk at an auction. I really fancied the trunk, only when I got home the trunk wasn't empty. It was full of old books and maps and I think that's where I got the sextant, and of course, the portrait. I emptied it out, and the contents are strewn about your room somewhere. I had every intention of investigating them, but . . . he came shortly after that.' Christina drifted off into the past, remembering a man called Gabriel who helped her to paint again.

'Snap out of it, Christina.' Mrs. Buck clicked her fingers. 'He was a pig. Men are pigs. Newton was a pig.'

She was on a 'men are swine' roll when Christina snorted, 'What about Stephen, huh? Is he a pig?'

'My husband,' Mrs. Buck smiled at her own good fortune, 'is one in a million. To be fair, he is more of a woman than a man, and that is very much to his advantage.'

The two women smiled in agreement here and for a moment Isadora Elzbeth tried to imagine Stephen Buck, Mrs. Buck's husband, but all she saw was a moustached man in a dress clutching a handbag. She let the image go and reverted back to her first question.

'So,' she persevered, 'is alchemy a branch of chemistry?'

Mrs. Buck slid back into her seat and became preoccupied with the view. Christina looked questioningly at the sky before answering.

'Let's see. What do I know about alchemy? It's a bogus science. It's not really science, but then again it's where science began. As far as I know, alchemy originated in the east. China. It's a secret science. They worked in secret and wrote in the most obscure way possible. They had laboratories with furnaces and they were constantly lighting white-hot fires trying to melt metals to turn them into gold. The fires were so hot that mythical creatures were supposed to flick out of the flames. Salamanders. Only these salamanders weren't like the ones in a river, I think they had wings on their backs. I'm not really sure. This looking for the "agent" that would turn base metals into gold was called looking for the Arcanum.'

Isadora Elzbeth nodded, she remembered what Sia had written.

'As far as I am aware, a good alchemist always had a grotty laboratory, filled with ridiculous things like antelopes' bladders and quicksilver. The first books on alchemy were written in Chinese. The whole science was tied in with magic. You've got to remember, this was a time before technology. The world was populated with weird superstitions, people believed in ghosts and angels, the air was thick with spirits back then.' Christina sipped her coffee. 'I suppose, when you think about it, if you watch one chemical blend and transform into another, it does look quite magical. We can analyse it all scientifically now, but back then, in their crude laboratories, it must have looked like something magical had taken place.'

Isadora Elzbeth imagined Sia experimenting with acid and jars of green liquid and then she thought of Will's eyes.

'Of course then there is the whole philosophical side to alchemy. Great philosophers the world over, since time began, have wanted to know what is the essence of life? They wanted to capture it, this thing, this essence that made everything live. If they could catch it, they believed they could be immortal. This side of alchemy was called looking for 'the philosopher's stone'.

Isadora Elzbeth thought of Marianne and her apple-flavoured liqueur. Poor Marianne had died. She'd invented a green drink that she believed would protect her and Will and Sia from the plague, but instead of living forever, she died. She must have been very disappointed.

'Then there's another story.' Christina wasn't finished.

'What do you do for pleasure?' Penguin took his head out of his dish where he was busily licking the cream off all the strawberries, 'swallow encyclopaedias? You have got to get out more.'

Christina rearranged the tiara on her head. 'It has something to do with a king in Saxony, and a young alchemist trying to find the Arcanum to make porcelain.'

'Augustus the Second,' Isadora Elzbeth remembered out loud.

'That's who it was.' Christina was surprised by Isadora Elzbeth's knowledge.

'I read it in the journal.'

'What's the weather forecast?' Mrs. Buck surprised them all by volunteering to get involved in the conversation.

'Good,' Christina piped. 'Look at the sky, it's as clear as you could wish for.'

'Except for the clouds,' Penguin contradicted.

Isadora Elzbeth stroked Penguin's ears and incorrectly translated. 'He wants to know how high up we'll go?'

'Actually, I am interested,' he agreed.

'A few hundred feet,' Christina informed them, 'maybe a thousand or two.'

Penguin wanted a measuring tape. He wanted to calculate how high two thousand feet was exactly.

'Shall we bring the telescope?'

'And maybe the kitchen sink?' Penguin suggested.

Mrs. Buck smiled. 'Show Christina how you plan on bringing him to the opening.'

Isadora Elzbeth obliged, explaining to Christina as she forced Penguin onto her shoulders, 'I think it would be better to carry him this way around the city, 'cause he wanders off sometimes, but this way, see, I can carry him without it being too awkward.'

Penguin stiffened and whined, 'If this little girl hadn't just lost her parents, believe me I wouldn't be up here! But I will look like a fool for her sake, so smirk at me all you like.'

This last remark drove the women into a maternal frenzy. They jumped up and kissed and stroked him, and cooed, 'Isn't that the sweetest thing? He has a heart after all. Pussy pussy cat, kiss kiss, slurp slurp!'

'You're pathetic. Get off, get off, both of you.' Penguin flicked his tale impatiently and ducked under Isadora Elzbeth's curls to avoid lipsticky lips.

The afternoon passed away in a haze of lazy sunshine and Gershwin songs. Mrs. Buck could play the guitar like Django Reinhardt.

'He had only three fingers on one hand, I don't know which one.' She held up her hand to make sure all her fingers were there. By mid-afternoon she was playing swing and she could sing too. She taught Isadora Elzbeth how to sing 'The Love Bug Will Bite You'.

'Come on, Penguin,' she called, 'this is Louis Prima at his best.'

Penguin swayed appreciatively and for a split second fell in love with Mrs. Buck. Christina danced the flamenco, even though it didn't quite go with the music, but it was the only dance she knew. In the noise and pleasantness of it all, Isadora Elzbeth actually managed to smile and sing and forget what had happened in her life during the last week.

Preparations for the famous voyage in the red balloon began at four o'clock. Mrs. Buck nudged Christina awake. A fit of flamenco had worn her out and she had decided to take a siesta among the soft folds of the deflated balloon. Mrs. Buck poked her with her toe, saying, 'Hey, Gitana! It's party time.'

Christina sat up all confused, then, looking at the sail-cloth billowing around her, she laughed.

'I had a dream that I was on a blood-red cloud travelling over an ice-blue sea, and I heard a man's voice say *You will know me when we meet again*.' She smiled a sleepy smile, unaware that her golden tiara had slipped sideways on her head.

Mrs. Buck wasn't paying any attention. She grabbed her handbag and descended into the living-room, where she blasted out sad Spanish music and sipped on thick espresso coffee.

'What time is it?' Christina asked Isadora Elzbeth.

'I heard the church bells strike four times.'

'Then it's four o'clock, and all is well. Right, let's get organised. We'll load the basket.'

Eleven

The next hour passed in a flurry of organisation. Marian was roused off the sofa and away from her Spanish dreams of Córdoba. Everyone joined forces preparing for the journey. The telescope was dismantled and reassembled inside the basket. They loaded cushions, maps, a barometer, a compass and a tin of sardines for Penguin to feast on. While Christina was busy attaching the burner to the base of the balloon, the others disappeared downstairs to get ready.

'This calls for Pachelbel or Sammartini,' Mrs. Buck said, hovering over the CD collection. 'No, no, something more grand, something with more trumpet in it. I've found it.' She whipped a CD from the pile. 'My dear friend Antonio, a concerto for lute, two violins and basso continuo in D major.' She cranked the CD up to full volume and Vivaldi blasted out loud regal music. In the chaos of the baroque tunes, Mrs. Buck dragged a full-length mirror out of Christina's bedroom and mimed instructions to Isadora Elzbeth.

'First,' she indicated, holding her index finger up as you would in a game of charades, 'me get into dress.' This was illustrated by her stepping into an invisible pool and then pulling something up over her wiggling hips. She turned in time to the music and began weaving her fingers all over her back before pointing at Isadora Elzbeth.

Penguin cocked his head to one side. 'Oh I get it! First she's going to go mad and then the men in white coats are going to tie her into a strait-jacket.'

Mrs. Buck took her dress off its hanger and, slipping out of her modern clothes, stepped into the orange folds of her costume. While Isadora Elzbeth fastened up the hooks and eyes, Penguin kept muttering things like, 'I wouldn't be bothered,' and 'Another little tug and we could cut off her oxygen supply. It's only an idea.'

At last Mrs. Buck was ready. She stepped into the middle of the room and Isadora Elzbeth thought how beautiful and at the same time how odd she looked. The burnt-orange silk made her skin look more sallow, the diamanté bodice glistened and the shards of light seemed to reflect in Mrs. Buck's eyes. Because the dress pulled her waist in and exaggerated her hips, she looked smaller, more fragile. The bodice did strange things to her bosom, and the white lace that frothed from the sleeves draped over her hands, making her fingers look precious and slender. For all this exotic beauty, Mrs. Buck looked faintly like a wind-up toy, a dream lady from the past who seemed oddly mechanical when she moved.

'It's in my way,' she shouted over the blaring music.

'Then turn it down,' Penguin howled back, misunderstanding her.

'They would have danced minuets and possibly galliards in these dresses back then.' Mrs. Buck did a little run on her tippy-toes, followed by a fabulous twist and two pointy kicks, only to stumble on the hem of her dress and end up clinging to the back of the sofa.

Penguin sniggered. 'Bet that was a popular dance.'

'Yes, well,' Mrs. Buck regained her composure and mouthed over the music, 'needs a bit of work. Your turn, Isadora Elzbeth.'

Isadora Elzbeth loved the dress. The silk slid through her hands. The stiff bodice, with its harlequin design of lime-green lozenges, pressed against her chest. The long slender sleeves had tiny puffs at the shoulders that were slashed to reveal emerald layers. The wide skirt felt airy and romantically foreign.

She stood looking at herself in the mirror. Inside the glass she saw a girl who could have been painted in a book of fairytales. A pale-faced girl with smoky-grey eyes who looked sharp and intelligent. A girl with dark curls falling in wisps over her shoulders. A girl who could not laugh, because there was a huge sorrow pressing on her heart.

'You look like a princess,' Christina whispered and Isadora Elzbeth jumped because she had seen only herself in the mirror.

Christina climbed into her purple-striped costume. While she was being fastened up she kept waving her hands and saying, 'Let them eat cake, fruit cake, any kind of cake, I don't care. Let them eat cake!'

'I'll have a cream puff,' Penguin interjected.

'I am pretending to be Marie Antoinette, the young and beautifully stupid queen of France.'

'I'm sure the stupid bit is right for you,' Penguin mused.

'Poor Marie Antoinette,' Christina said, drifting over to turn the music down, 'she will only ever be remembered for that facile phrase, "Let them eat cake". Lost her head to Madame la Guillotine. But her mother was very interesting, Marie Theresa of Austria, ascended to the throne at the tender age of twenty-three. She was beautiful, with golden hair; loved to play cards and dance all night; was madly in love with her husband, who was a bit of a dull man, not terribly bright, very unfaithful, constantly had affairs, I think his name was Fredrick...'

'Oh God, spare me. Not another stunning biographical tale from Madame encyclopaedia over there.' Penguin cried fake tears into his paws.

Christina laughed off Penguin's remark. She seemed to be able to move freely in her gown. She stooped down to tie her bootlaces, only to stand up all puffy-faced.

'You know what I've discovered?'

'That pilchards and sardines are most delicious on toast?' Penguin enquired hungrily.

'That you can't breathe and tie your boots at the same

time in these dresses.' She hoisted her foot onto the back of the sofa and asked Mrs. Buck to do the honours. 'No wonder they had maids back then. Still,' Christina became wistful, 'it must have been very enchanting to live in those days. When people curtseyed, and everyone was very courtly. When there was etiquette, and women were loved for their grace and being demure and ladylike.'

'When was the last time you were demure?' Mrs. Buck butted in. 'Hark at her! Miss 'I'll punch any man that annoys me' is dreaming of being demure. Good God, a thousand kingdoms would topple before you'd ever be demure.

'Yes, all right,' Christina snapped.

'Hah!' Mrs. Buck wouldn't let it drop. 'You'd have to chop her head off before she'd become demure!' The argument continued as they locked up and climbed the stairs to the roof. 'And another thing,' Mrs. Buck ranted, 'I can't believe you are romancing about the good old baroque days. You know damn well, Christina, they were barbaric times, except of course for the music. Then there were fabulous composers, Telemann, Bach, Handel.'

'Oh of course, the music is always sophisticated,' Christina parried, 'people slicing each other's heads off in between writing concertos. You don't see a flaw in your argument anywhere, do you?'

'They were ignorant times, Christina, and times that women did not fare well in, I might add. Besides, you know that music transcends everything.'

'Oh really? And what about the paintings? Velázquez

and Watteau, Fragonard and Tiepolo. And the architecture, Pöppelmann and Bernini?'

'All those artists are from different centuries.'

Christina turned and stamped her foot on the landing. She huffed through her nose, but pursed her lips tight because she knew Mrs. Buck was right. The women continued on up the stairs, their elegant gowns flowing over the rickety steps, their argument turning to dowries and how a woman's only career option was marriage or piracy. Isadora Elzbeth picked Penguin up and squashed him onto her shoulders.

'Oh bloody hell,' he moaned, but Isadora Elzbeth thought he was pleased and she rubbed foreheads with him, saying, 'I love you too.' As she turned to follow the others, something in the garden below caught her eye. She crept nearer the window and, through the grime, saw someone standing beneath the lilac trees. He stepped forward and looked at her. A dark man in a black suit. He didn't wave or nod his head, but Isadora Elzbeth knew he had seen her, because he turned his face so deliberately towards the window where she stood. Above him, in the pale evening sky, was the thin gleam of a new moon. She shivered and stepped back into the shadows and murmured at Penguin, 'The man Marianne saw.' Then she shook her head. 'No, that can't be. It was over two hundred years ago. Of course he's not the same man.' She looked down into the garden again, but he was gone. There was an empty place filled with green shadows where he had once been.

Disturbed by what she had seen, Isadora Elzbeth kept

it to herself and made her way in preoccupied silence to the balcony. She was glad to step into the warm sunshine. The noise of the city washed over her, a radio blared in the distance. Over the chug of the traffic she could hear the rhythm of workmen hammering. She checked the lilac trees again. No one stood underneath them.

Isadora Elzbeth climbed to the roof and gasped at the shock of the sight before her. The balloon was enormous. It towered over the roof, a voluminous scarlet ball that blotted out half the sky. Christina and Mrs. Buck were giggling inside the basket, waving at the people below who were leaning out of the windows of the taxi-rank offices to take a look at the extraordinary sight. Isadora Elzbeth felt the unexpected thrill of adventure tingle in her bones. 'Anything can happen, Penguin,' she whispered, 'absolutely anything!'

She climbed into the basket and felt her stomach swirl inside her. Christina tugged on the burner and a hiss of blue flame pushed hot air inside the balloon. Mrs. Buck untied the ropes and threw down the sandbags. The crowd gathering below cheered. Isadora Elzbeth held onto the basket until her knuckles were white. She felt light-headed and giddy.

The balloon jerked and bounced along the roof, until one long gaseous hiss drove the balloon up in a slow gentle curve, over the rooftops and sideways along Wexford Street. Magically weightless they floated above the city, over the triangular rooftops, over pathways and gardens and winding roads. The traffic had come to a standstill, passengers got out of their cars and waved up to them and Mrs. Buck waved back and encouraged Penguin to come and see. Penguin peeped over the side to say 'Thank you, I love you all,' but the sudden height made him feel dizzy, so he lay down and moaned about vertigo.

Up and up the balloon went, in a slow vertical glide that made Isadora Elzbeth's tummy sink and rise as they bobbed over the air currents. The view was spectacular.

Christina laughed loudly. 'Isn't this amazing. The world's shrunk. The world's upside down. All tiny, itsy-bitsy upside downy world.'

'I think she may be inhaling too many fumes,' Penguin said seriously.

'The wind is from the south-west, which is absolutely perfect because that's the direction we want to go in.'

Mrs. Buck didn't get it. If the wind was from the south-west, did that mean they were being pushed to the north-east? Does a wind push you in the direction from which it comes or in the opposite direction? Obviously it must be the opposite direction, which must mean the wind was blowing from the north-east. Christina tried to work it out on a piece of paper.

'Oh dear God.' Penguin was getting a headache. 'They'd confuse Vasco da Gama. They couldn't navigate themselves out of a driveway. Who let them into this balloon?'

'Of course we're going north-east if the wind is from the south-west,' Christina finally figured.

Mrs. Buck 'but-ed' her: 'But, if that's the case,

according to this map the Royal Hospital in Kilmainham is to the south.'

Christina grabbed the map and then, frowning, decided it didn't matter where anything was because they were going in the right direction, and that was all that mattered, everything else was superfluous. She tugged on the burner and the balloon sailed over St. Patrick's Cathedral. Isadora Elzbeth loved the Gothic church, with its spidery buttresses and long pointy windows. As they rose higher to avoid the spire, Isadora Elzbeth said she could smell the clouds. 'They smell of primrose and watermint'. Mrs. Buck and Christina gulped in the air, but after three breaths said that all they could smell was the hops from the Guinness brewery.

'You see back there,' Christina leaped away from the burner and pointed back to St. Patrick's park, 'where those circular flower-beds are? Two hundred and fifty years ago there were houses where those flower-beds are now. Tenements, leaning in on top of one another, practically built up to the cathedral steps. The place was crawling with kids. It was very, very poor. The kids used to call the Dean names – Dean Swift, that is, a very famous writer. He had a long-time girlfriend called Stella. His worst fear was that he would go mad, and of course the supreme irony was that he did go mad. They locked him away in a mental asylum. I'm not sure if I'd have liked him; he was a ditherer, hated making decisions. He had a solution to the starvation problem in Dublin back then. He suggested that the hungry roast their children and eat them! He didn't really mean it, though. He had what's called a satirical sense of humour. He was the master of satire.'

'Your talent for digression is astounding.' Penguin leaned against the side of the basket. Beneath his fur he was pale with travel sickness. 'I know what Swift would want to do with you, he'd want to stew your head.'

'Oh look, now this is perfect.' Christina bounced over to the other side of the basket. 'Coming up, below us, is Thomas Street. There's that famous building where Robert Emmet was hung, drawn and quartered.' Christina's face pinched up in disgust. 'You don't want to know what that involves.'

'I'll hazard a guess,' Penguin commented dryly. 'First you're hung, then you're drawn and, correct me if I'm wrong here, then you're quartered.'

'Can you see that cupola in the distance? That little bell-tower feature and that long rectangular roof? That's the museum. It was originally built as a hospital for soldiers. I don't know anything else about it, I'm afraid.'

'Thank God for that,' Penguin sighed. 'Now perhaps you'll stop gibbering and pull on the burner. My stomach is sinking, I think we're losing altitude.'

Christina tugged on the burner and a blast of hot air pushed them suddenly higher. Mrs. Buck examined the distant quays through the telescope while Christina went on talking.

'Actually, the word "gibberish" is interesting.' Penguin could still be shocked by the fact that his comments were understood. He looked sulkily at the strawberries and restrained himself from making any further sarcastic remarks. 'Isadora Elzbeth, this will interest you. The word gibberish is derived from the name of an Arab alchemist called Jabir. His writings were such jumbled-up nonsense that people began to use his name whenever they were trying to describe something that made absolutely no sense. It's interesting, isn't it?'

Isadora Elzbeth nodded. She was worried about Penguin; he seemed unnaturally quiet. Christina was pointing to domes and spires, calling out names and telling interesting stories. 'That's where the woman with one eye fell in love with a man half her age. She paralysed him with a love potion which had arsenic in it. Arsenic, I ask you! Didn't Rasputin build up his immunity to poison by eating minuscule amounts of arsenic? It's mostly used for rat poison now. People were quite ignorant back then. I know that they put arsenic into paint long ago. I remember seeing wallpaper, it had been designed by Morris, that had arsenic in it. It was deep-green paper fading to black. People died from the toxicity of the paper. It's a bit of a stupid way to die. Imagine being killed by wallpaper.'

Christina was mostly talking to herself while Mrs. Buck and Isadora Elzbeth silently shared the telescope. Through the tiny eye-piece Isadora Elzbeth saw far away things zooming right up under her nose. The distant traffic crossing the bridge was brought up close enough to see the people inside the cars. Isadora Elzbeth saw lawyers with black cloaks and wigs running up the steps of the Four Courts, she saw statues with birds perched on top of their heads, she saw market stalls, archaeologists digging, cranes craning and workmen building. She saw all of this from far away, riding over their heads.

This is what a moth can see when it flies to the moon. Only there are no moths in the city, she thought, and her mind drifted back to the pear tree in her garden and the full, bitter-sweet moon that she and Penguin used to sing under.

'We're almost there, a couple more blasts should do it.' Christina tugged on the burner and Penguin, who had slowly gained confidence, rose and gave a tentative sniff over the edge of the basket.

'I can think of better ways of seeing the world,' he complained, 'though I suppose it is interesting to see it from a bird's point of view.' He looked at the passing birds and felt hungry.

Christina told a story about how she had once found an article written over one hundred years ago by a surgeon. 'He and his doctor friend, I'll never forget the name, Dr. Grimshaw. I wouldn't like a visit from a doctor called Grimshaw. With a name like that he's bound to amputate something. Anyway, they went walking around Dublin in the late 1800s and his descriptions were vile. He talks of tenements that had a few planks of wood by way of a door, and every room was dingy and crammed with people. No toilets, an ash-pit in the front for everyone to use, chickens and pigs kept in makeshift pens in any available space. But the interesting thing was the amount of manure. He described a mountain of it piled fifty feet high, twenty feet deep and sixty feet long in an alleyway down by the Coombe. He said it was so near the houses that he couldn't understand how half the population hadn't contracted typhoid or cholera, or just dropped dead on the spot from the stench of the stuff. There were cesspools and poisonous streams running in rills along the road. He said the river Poddle was a thick black gloop of muck and manure and that he saw one woman go down with a bucket to take some of the water!'

Penguin made a sour face, he was beginning to find Christina's rants interesting.

'Nearly there,' Christina said.

'Then what happened?' Penguin assumed there was a point to the story.

'There's Heuston station, where we came in.' Mrs. Buck was no longer at the telescope, she was holding one of the ropes and leaning slightly over to get a better view of everything beneath her. Her silk dress rippled in the soft breeze, her hair pushed away from her face, and she was smiling. In her pretty dress, with her bright brown eyes, she looked girlish.

The balloon drifted over a walled park with lush, fat trees, and the traces of an old garden long abandoned. In the centre of the park there was a rectangular building, grey and coldly elegant. Despite the fact that it was now the Irish Museum of Modern Art, it still had that sombre feeling of an abandoned hospital. As the moment of arrival drew nearer, Christina and Mrs. Buck became more fussed. They fluffed up their hair, touched up their lipstick, became technical about managing the balloon.

'We want to glide down,' Mrs. Buck insisted, 'gracefully, not disgracefully, Christina. A certain regal descent, with lots of elegance. Then I'll squirt the champagne. And once we've landed smoothly Johannes will scoop us up out of the basket. After all, he likes scooping women up, carrying them off in his big brawny arms.'

'He'll probably flip us over his shoulders,' Christina giggled as she manoeuvred the balloon over the blue-pitched roof of the hospital.

'Not in these dresses he won't!' Mrs. Buck had the champagne bottle by the neck and was scraping the gold foil away from the cork. Her cheeks were spotted with pink and her eyes had a giddy sparkle in them. Now that they were almost there, Isadora Elzbeth felt suddenly nervous. She had forgotten that there would be lots of people at Johannes Handley's opening. Strangers looking up at her. She felt horribly self-conscious and began to wish they would just sail on over the crowd and land discreetly in the garden and maybe stay there and not bother anybody. But it was too late. The balloon sailed over the dainty cupola and Christina managed to steady it over the courtyard, where gasps drifted up from the people below.

Christina and Mrs. Buck waved brashly at the crowd. A sea of hands waved back. There were so many people! Men dressed in black, women in flowing dresses with thin shoulder straps. They all held glasses of wine in one hand and blocked the sun from their eyes with the other. There must have been seven hundred people gathered. Scattered among them, displayed in careful positions, were Johannes

Handley's sculptures, but no one was paying any attention to them. As the balloon descended with just the right amount of elegance and grace, Isadora Elzbeth began to make out individual faces. They were hard-to-impress faces, faces that were spoilt and demanding, faces that were tired of ordinary things. Yet for the moment they were surprised by the sight of a red balloon carrying two baroque ladies, an elfin-looking girl and a queasy cat.

An excited flurry buzzed through the crowd, a murmur, a parting in the sea of people. A strong handsome man with dark hair and a scarlet jacket moved through the crowd and tilted his head upward. It was Johannes Handley, smiling broadly. As the balloon came nearer and he could make out Christina and Mrs. Buck, he blew them slow tender kisses, one each, with a broad sweep of his right hand.

Christina flushed slightly and for a moment seemed shy. Then regaining her composure she called down, loud enough for everyone to hear, 'I am Scarlet and Airborne. What is your reply?'

A boom of laughter rose from the crowd. Johannes Handley got the joke, and joined in the applause that burst out of the crowd. Penguin became more brave. He leaned over the side and, stretching out one paw, said, 'Thank you, I love you,' and then to Isadora Elzbeth he said, 'I came, I saw, I conquered.' The press photographers clicked and flashed and clucked – around the balloon first, and then Johannes Handley. As the balloon descended steadily the crowd parted. Johannes Handley stood alone and raised his glass to the women.

101

'I salute the better artists,' he called up.

Christina and Mrs. Buck smiled modestly. Isadora Elzbeth realised they hadn't spoiled his show after all. Instead, they had given Johannes Handley a precious gift, something every artist needs. Publicity! And plenty of it. The women didn't care that the crowd thought that Johannes Handley had engineered the whole thing. They were his friends, they liked to keep him on his toes, punch him in the eye when they had to and support him flamboyantly when necessary. The balloon hovered above the crowd. Mrs. Buck insisted on Christina steadying it just so she could give the Gutterscot Gallery crowd a good soaking. The cork shot out of the champagne bottle with a crack, and a spray of white foam sent the onlookers shrieking for shelter. Johannes Handley extended his arms, tilted his head back and opened his mouth, the balloon hovering above his head. This was the photograph that made the front page, an ecstatic, champagne-soaked artist, dripping with victory. Isadora Elzbeth felt happy for the success they had brought. She hoisted Penguin onto her shoulders, and he screeched his protest into her ears.

'I think so too,' she replied, nuzzling into his face. 'It's been a lovely adventure.' All Penguin could do was sigh and slump in a huff around her neck.

'Come on down,' the crowd shouted.

Christina fussed about and laughed. She twisted the temperature gauge on the burner, called down to her friends and gulped champagne, until finally she turned to Mrs. Buck and said, 'I'm not too sure if this can be done elegantly. In fact, I'm not too sure if this can be done at all.'

'Oh, put it down anyway.' Mrs. Buck flipped her hands and liked the way the lace flopped over her fingers. Christina twisted the handle on the burner, which unexpectedly sent the balloon shooting towards the clock tower. The crowd ran after them shouting instructions. Mrs. Buck pushed Christina out of the way and guided the balloon with speedy accuracy straight towards the stable walls.

'Collision is imminent,' Penguin roared over the din at Isadora Elzbeth. 'I said so, I said they couldn't navigate their way out of a driveway. They are going to kill us. The only option is to jump.'

While Penguin mulled over the choices available to him, the balloon swung from one end of the courtyard to the other. Isadora Elzbeth tried not to panic, but the crowd rushing about screaming below them didn't help. She clung to the side of the basket and tried to steady the telescope as it toppled over and smashed into the strawberries. Christina brought the balloon up, and it steadied for a moment. There was applause from below, then the noise was blotted out by a gust of wind. A frisky south-westerly snatched the balloon and pushed it quickly upwards and outwards. Mrs. Buck was thrown against the ropes, Christina's feet were pulled from under her and she sprawled on the basket floor, and Isadora Elzbeth dived for the burner. The balloon grazed the topmost branches of the fat trees, and a whirl of birds flapped crossly up into the air. It was useless, the balloon was pulled higher and further by the blustering winds. Down below the shrinking crowd rushed after them.

There was nothing Isadora Elzbeth could do except hang on for dear life. The wind was no longer skittish, it was vigorous and wild, menacingly sucking them further away from the earth, dragging them higher into the blasting, cold geospheric winds. The balloon was tossed like a weightless red toy, over the clouds, out over the city and towards the grey swell of the Irish Sea.

Christina and Mrs. Buck looked sick with terror, frozen as they gripped the side of the basket. Isadora Elzbeth tried to let go of the burner, but her fingers were numb. She swayed with every toss of the balloon. Penguin's claws were embedded in her skirt. The sea was coming towards them quickly, the grim empty horizon waiting to swallow them up, and still the balloon rose higher.

Mrs. Buck called out, her eyes wide with horror, 'Don't let go.'

Her voice battled through the gulping wind. Clouds were rolling in from America, deep brooding clouds, soft and treacherous as a lion's paw. There was nothing beneath them now but the puckered surface of the sea, nothing to save them if they went down. Isadora Elzbeth closed her eyes. The balloon rocked and bounced with the wind. She heard Christina cry out and when she opened her eyes she saw nothing but the foggy, grey interior of a cloud.

'Are you still here?' she yelled, but the question was punched to the moon. For just then the wind veered and knocked her back so viciously that her fingers slid from the metal handle of the burner. Her back slammed into the side of the basket, and she grabbed mutely at the air, but there was nothing to hold on to. She was flicked backwards, out into the sky, falling, tumbling over and under, into a seamless grey horror. She tried to cry for her mother, but only the word 'moth' came out.

Twelve

The Silvery Water and the Starry Earth

Mariya also said: The 'water' which I have mentioned is an angel,
and descends from the sky, and the earth accepts it
on account of its moistness.
So says Mariya and she meant by this:
*The child which they say will be
born for them in the air.*

*From the writings of Ibn Umail on the Alchemist Writings of Maria the
Jewess*

Isadora Elzbeth felt the awful rush of descent. Her
lungs stretched, her arms reached, her legs kicked, her
heart clawed up along her ribs. She twisted over and under,
aware of a red-hot pain searing her thigh. Penguin was rip-
ping her flesh to shreds, desperately trying to stay with her.
They sped through the nightmare of the cloud, accelerat-
ing through the atmosphere, gulping for breath.

Down and down they fell, faster and faster, through
the booming loudness of the wind, until suddenly they
were clear of the cloud and Isadora Elzbeth could see the

horror of the fate that awaited her. She wasn't going to plummet into the ice-cold waters of the Irish Sea. Instead she was going to hit earth; she was falling towards a brown flat land, aware as she spun hopelessly to her death that there were snow-capped mountains and alpine forests circling her. She cried out as the earth came quickly towards her, a hopeless awful scream, and then smack! The world went black.

She never knew what happened in that darkness. Missed minutes or hours that could never be recovered. All she knew was that she woke up, sick and sore and groggy, to the sound of a beautiful voice.

'I saw you, cast out of heaven like a fallen angel. I am glad that you are not dead, because I want to know how you can fly.'

Isadora Elzbeth opened her eyes; even her lids ached. She was in stiff, damp pain, every bone in her body hurt. She stared upwards, slowly recollecting everything. There was no rain-cloud above her. There was a clear evening sky, tinged with a deep blue that seemed to go on for ever.

'I was standing on my roof. I saw the spectacle – of course, I didn't know you were a little girl – but I saw something hurtling out of space towards Gabriel's Peak and I had to come to see.'

The voice was mellifluous, a woman's voice, and it came over the brown heads of the bulrushes that swayed in the evening breeze. The woman was somewhere beside Isadora Elzbeth. She was on her knees, opening something. Then her hands felt along Isadora Elzbeth's body.

'Curl your toes,' she said.

Isadora Elzbeth curled her toes and felt slime squeeze through them. Where are my shoes? she thought.

'You'll be sore,' the voice continued, 'but miraculously there's nothing broken. I am going to put three drops from a vial onto your lips. Sip it, and lie still while it takes effect.'

A glass tube with greenish liquid appeared under Isadora Elzbeth's nose, and three drops the shape of tears plopped onto her lips and slid along her tongue, down her throat and straight to her heart. It tasted of apple, and burned with a phosphorous heat that travelled from the tips of her fingers to the soles of her feet. The woman moved, and Isadora Elzbeth heard her slurping through the marsh.

'Poor cat,' the soft voice said. 'Nine lives, and a tale to tell. Raise your head, poor creature.' She must have given Penguin the same liquid, because Isadora Elzbeth heard him meow. A tear shot out from the corner of her eye because she was so happy he was not dead.

'Well, how are you feeling?' The woman leaned over her and at last Isadora Elzbeth could put a face to the voice. It was not a beautiful face. It did not match the voice. It was a manly face, a large awkward face of jumbled features, the most striking of which were the pale, opalescent eyes. She had large eyebrows, a wide nose, a long full mouth, enormous cheekbones that protruded too much and a full square chin. She had long, shiny brown hair that was plaited and tied up in elaborate swirls. But it was her eyes that Isadora Elzbeth was faintly scared by, they seemed to have a bit of the moon in them.

'Hello.' She smiled a lop-sided smile. 'Can you remember your name, fallen angel?'

Isadora Elzbeth tried to smile back, but it hurt. 'My name is Isadora Elzbeth.'

'The girl with two names,' the woman said. 'My name is Ambrosia. My father had been reading classical legends at the time when I was born, and decided to call me after an ancient foodstuff that was supposed to bestow immortality. Everyone calls me Sia. I'm going to try to extract you from the marsh now. I've pulled your cat out.'

Penguin walked gingerly over to Isadora Elzbeth and licked her cheek. Sia reached under Isadora Elzbeth's neck with one arm, and behind her knees with the other. She was a big, strong woman. There was a loud sucking noise as she lifted Isadora Elzbeth up.

'There,' Sia said, 'unstuck from the glue.'

Isadora Elzbeth rested her head on Sia's broad shoulder. She was dazed and confused, but she left her head empty and did nothing but look around her at the world over the bump of Sia's shoulder. A circle of drooping larch trees surrounded the marsh, and behind them a ring of snow-capped mountains pointed towards the evening stars. A sickle moon, wafer-thin, hung like an anchor above the highest peak. She watched the darkness creep in from the east, her eyes fascinated by the moon, and then she saw him, moving out of the darkness along the edge of the trees, over the marsh, following them. The Darkman. The same man who had watched her from under the lilac trees in 30 Wexford Street. She recognised him because he had the same form. A nobleness in the tilt of his head, a strength in the breadth of his shoulders. He had the subtlety of a stalking beast, watchful, ready to spring. Patient. He moved stealthily, a silhouette in the approaching darkness.

It was only later, when she told Penguin everything, that she wondered if she was alive or dead. 'Because it cannot be! We've fallen into the pages of a book, a journal written over two hundred years ago. And the Darkman stalking us couldn't possibly have travelled here unless he's a ghost. Do you think we're dead?' she asked Penguin as she sat at the window of the bedroom Sia had put her in. 'If we are dead, then how come the Darkman is haunting us? Can the dead be haunted by ghosts?'

She leaned back and remembered everything. How Sia had carried her all the way home, over two miles. How she had rested only once. How kind and talkative she was, pausing to wait for Penguin to catch up. And every time Sia stopped, the Darkman melted into the shadows and reappeared when only Isadora Elzbeth could see him. Sia carried her across fields, over stiles, onto a twisting old road and eventually through a gate that opened into a fantastic garden with hedges cut into animal shapes, birds, dragons, cats, and even elephants. Cherry-coloured flowers sprouted beneath the menagerie hedges, blooms of lavender and orange blossom, red-hot pokers, irises and orchids grew in thick clumps in the flower-beds. The Darkman had not come through the gate. He had stayed far behind, until eventually the distance swallowed him up, leaving Isadora Elzbeth with one certainty, he was out there waiting.

The garden surrounded a house with a pitched roof and small windows. Its main structure was of wood, but there was an ornate granite doorway with an inscription carved into it which Isadora Elzbeth didn't have time to read until the next day. Inside, the house was warm and dim, oddly large and strangely empty. There was a huge open fire and elegant door frames fixed with classical mouldings. Sia had put her lying on a velvet-covered chaise-longue, leaving her alone for a few moments. In that time Isadora Elzbeth inspected the room; no detail escaped her eyes. Large cupboards pressed against the walls, some with glass doors, others sealed with hard wood. On the shelves of the glass cabinets were row after row of brass implements, jars and receptacles with spouts and handles. Liquid-preserved plants with thick roots were lined together and labelled on one shelf. There were books against the other wall, stacked from ceiling to floor. In the centre of the room there was a single dark table and two large chairs covered in red velvet, with gold curly feet and arms. A small picture hung over the fireplace. The walls were white. The window beneath which Isadora Elzbeth lay on the chaise-longue was open, and through it drifted the song of a nightingale. Penguin curled onto her lap. He purred quietly, humbled and exhausted by the fall.

'Only candlelight,' Isadora Elzbeth whispered into his sleeping ear, and she looked at the four candles – two above the mantelpiece, the other in large ornate holders on the table – and she knew in her heart something was wrong with the place. But it wasn't until later, when she was alone with Penguin, that she spoke what was in her heart.

Sia returned with a bowl of soup. She was an extremely tall woman, a large presence. She wore a long green dress, tailored simply with a square neck. In the candlelight her features were muted slightly. Isadora Elzbeth decided that her first impressions of Sia were probably a bit harsh. Her cheekbones were high and sharp, her eyes too pale, her mouth too long, but the combination of her features was more interesting and attractive then she had first thought. Sia was unusual looking, there was something faintly Egyptian about her. Despite the fact that she was large, she moved gracefully, and although her voice was big, it was beautifully resonant and animated with curiosity.

'I can't believe you haven't broken anything. You'll be badly bruised, but in a few days' time you'll be fine. Here, some broth. So, Isadora Elzbeth, the girl with two names, can you tell me how come you were up in the sky?'

'We were flying to a show. Penguin, Christina, Marian and I.' She sipped on the broth and thought for a moment. 'They could have fallen too,' she gasped, suddenly horrified.

'You were the only one who fell from the cloud,' Sia assured her. 'So your friends can fly too? What kind of engine takes you up?'

'I think Christina bought it in an antique shop. It was a hot-air balloon, it carried us right over Dublin City, to the hospital where the show was.'

'A hot-air balloon? This is your flying machine? How does it work?'

Isadora Elzbeth felt a chill fingering her spine; she told Penguin why later.

'It's sailcloth, sewn together into a huge circle, almost closed at one end, then hot air is pumped inside it and it fills out and begins to rise. It's attached to a basket and it flies.'

Sia smiled and confounded Isadora Elzbeth by saying, 'I knew that! Look, I have one in miniature here.' She opened one of the cupboards and produced a beautifully decorated toy balloon. She placed it over a candle and the little balloon filled out and rose up. It hovered above the heat while Isadora Elzbeth looked at it eerily suspended, a tiny version of the contraption she had just fallen from, and all she could think was, 'Where am I?'

'Are there many balloons in Dublin?' Sia turned one of the large red chairs towards the window and blinked her moon-filled eyes as she waited for the answer.

'I don't think so,' Isadora Elzbeth replied.

'Probably too expensive to run,' Sia volunteered. 'Is Dublin far from here?'

Isadora Elzbeth could only nod her head. She wanted to say, 'It's over two hundred years away,' but she was afraid that Sia would think she was mad and have her put into an asylum, like the Dean of St. Patrick's Cathedral, Mr. Swift.

'Let's not worry about the distance,' Sia said, unravelling her long plaits, 'we'll get you home somehow. Perhaps your friends will come and fetch you anyway. For the moment you must rest, give the liqueur time to restore you. It's quiet here. I try to visit the city as little as possible. I work in the garden. Do you like flowers?'

Isadora Elzbeth nodded.

'You can help me then. I'll give you gentle work. After a fall like that I'm sure you'll be fit for nothing but watching. I hope you don't mind me observing, but your colouring is very foreign. Have you Spanish blood in you?'

Isadora Elzbeth thought of her mother's black hair and sadly shook her head.

'I once met a Spanish nobleman with a French name. Have you heard of the Count of Saint-Germain? No? He has dark hair, raven black like yours, and eyes the colour of slate, full of secrets. He was very charming. I almost fell in love with him myself.'

Sia's hair was loose now, it flowed in ripples over her shoulders and framed her face, making her look exotic, an ugly person verging on extreme beauty. Isadora Elzbeth tried to guess how old Sia was; she was beyond her twenties, in her early thirties maybe.

'Your eyes hold the same expression as the Count's. Perhaps you are related?' Sia leaned forward, her smile was big and generous, 'And if you are related to the Count of Saint-Germain, then perhaps you possess some of his talents?'

Isadora Elzbeth felt disappointed. She'd have liked to have been related to the Comte, for Sia's sake, but she shook her head.

Sia's laugh rolled out into the room. 'Don't look so sad,' she said, 'I am certain the Comte is a talented spy, and all his magical claims are nothing but an elaborate front to procure monies from stupid aristocrats.'

'He's a magician?' Isadora Elzbeth asked.

'A wizard,' Sia said smiling, 'claims to be thousands of years old. But I liked him. We discussed experiments and he showed me how to make dyes, very beautiful colours.' Sia looked towards the window and her pale blue eyes remembered something that seemed to rest in the silent night outside.

'I'll shut that window for you, a draught could give you discomfort in your neck.' She curved over Isadora Elzbeth and pulled the window shut. 'It's early yet, but you seem tired. Would you like to sleep?'

Isadora Elzbeth nodded and Sia scooped her up and carried her through a blue door, along a corridor, up a dark stairwell and into a pitch-black room.

'I know this house like a blind woman.' Sia's voice spoke quietly above her. She eased Isadora Elzbeth down onto something soft and moved away. There was a scratching noise, then a small light flared from the other side of the room. Sia was bent over a small dresser lighting a candle. She brought it towards Isadora Elzbeth saying, 'This is my little sister's room. You'd better get out of your dress. Here.'

She placed the candle on the bedside locker and reached under the pillow, pulling out a nightdress. Two mothballs rolled out along the floor and Penguin thought about eating one of them. The pungent smell of lavender put him off that idea.

Sia pulled back the curtains, letting the starlight trickle in. She opened the window and perfume from the garden cleansed the musty air of the room. Isadora Elzbeth

115

needed help unhooking her dress. She pulled the muslin nightdress over her head and felt sore after she'd stretched up.

'We can talk tomorrow,' Sia said. 'I hope you sleep well. I know your muscles and bones will ache, but I have an ointment that will alleviate the pain. See you and your cat in the morning. By the way, I am next door if you need me. Until daylight then.'

She turned gracefully and strode out of the room, leaving Isadora Elzbeth to explain everything to Penguin.

'I don't know what happened,' Isadora Elzbeth said later, as she sat on the window seat looking at the stars and letting the fresh night air cool her. 'But somehow we've travelled through time. It's as though we pierced through a time bubble. I think that's what we've done. When we fell out of the balloon we punctured some kind of time bubble and now we're in the past.'

She stroked the length of Penguin's back; he was asleep on her lap.

'I don't understand how we should end up here though. In the place talked about in the journal. I don't understand how we should end up here, in this exact place, with Sia. It must be the year 1765, because that was the date on Journal X, after Marianne died, because this is Marianne's room.'

Isadora Elzbeth shook her head. It all seemed impossible to her.

'How can I be alive in the past?' she asked, then she wondered if she was dead, and then she remembered something that Marianne had said to Sia, '*The living are always changing places with the dead!*'

She began to cry quietly, because she was horribly con-fused. Nothing made sense, and the nonsense upset her. She went to bed, falling into a lonely sleep, long and deep and empty as for ever.

⊚ Thirteen

Yes for all the four corners of the world,
Morning, Evening, Midday and Midnight,
The angels which rule the four winds
Will bring you together.

From 'Uraltes Chymisches Werck' by the Alchemist
Abraham Eleazar, 1735

Isadora Elzbeth's lids snapped back. She was suddenly awake.

'It is the year 1765 and I am in trouble,' she whispered. She lay looking at the pale ceiling, turning over solutions inside her head.

'Sia is going to ask me so many questions, and I'll have to have an answer, but if I start telling her about the twentieth century she's going to think I'm mad.' Isadora Elzbeth lay for a long time trying to figure out what to do. In the end she decided to pretend.

'I'll pretend to have lost my memory; it will stall her. In the meantime, I'm going to have to try and find some way out of here.'

She tried to sit up, but every muscle in her body ached with pain. Sliding up slowly, she propped herself onto her pillow.

Marianne's room looked bigger in daylight. It was a simple room, painted a soft lavender colour, with a dark varnished wooden floor. There was hardly any furniture in it – a small dresser, the bed, and a thick black wardrobe that had long drawers at the bottom. Penguin was sitting on the window seat looking out of the open window. Someone was working in the garden. Every now and again a slicing metallic noise chopped through the air.

'There's a beautiful sweet smell of wild roses,' Isadora Elzbeth said to Penguin.

The cat turned his head slowly and blinked with disgust. 'Oh so you're awake are you? That's all fine and dandy. You wouldn't wake up when I wanted you to, would you? I practically jumped up and down on your chest, trampolining about the bed like an idiot, but oh no, you'd sleep through it all. Now you wake up, when it's not important.'

Penguin twitched his ears and turned away. Isadora Elzbeth stared at him, wishing she could decipher his meows. Then, supposing she was on the right track, she said, 'I realise we have a problem and I'll figure a way out. But for the moment we must keep these things to ourselves, no telling anyone. It's a mess, but don't you think,' she added cryptically, 'maybe we were all brought together, brought here, for a reason?'

Penguin shook his head and began cleaning his face.

119

'Come on,' Isadora Elzbeth said, carefully getting out of the large bed and gently lifting him up, 'let's go and see what the world was like hundreds of years ago.'

They walked along a wide sombre corridor and down the broad wooden stairs, past a grand old standing clock that had a picture painted on its face. Isadora Elzbeth stopped to see what time it was. Almost midday! She was shocked; she had slept for at least fifteen hours.

Penguin was in agony. 'If you'd just put me down,' he complained and Isadora Elzbeth nodded pensively, saying, 'I noticed it too. The painting on the clock is the same kind of ship as the one in Uncle Silas's globe.'

The front door was open and, when she stepped out into the garden, the blazing sunshine made her squint. Sia was trimming her hedges, she stepped out from behind a leafy dragon and smiled her long, crooked smile.

'At last. I thought you'd slipped into a coma. How are you?'

Isadora Elzbeth smiled and nodded. 'I'm a bit sore.'

'I bet you are.' Sia dropped her shears and pulled the green scarf she had been wearing off her head. Her thick brown hair collapsed over her shoulders. 'And I bet you're starving.'

She strode forward and Isadora Elzbeth thought of a tree in motion. Sia was wearing an olive-green dress; it clung to her waist and bosom and arms, it flowed down over her hips, that swayed a little when she moved. Nothing could diminish the size of Sia. She was monumental, statuesque. Large and solid like a tree.

'How's our feline friend doing?' she enquired, scratching under Penguin's chin.

'I think Penguin is a bit sore and hungry as well,' Isadora Elzbeth replied.

Sia laughed and went ahead inside.

Isadora Elzbeth followed her into the kitchen. Everything about the house was so foreign, the heavy wooden interior, the waxy smells, the bulky furniture, the sparseness of it all. The kitchen had a floor of black-and-white diamond tiles, a huge iron range, thick iron cauldrons, pans hanging from S-shaped hooks, a heavy pine table and two chairs. The window looked out onto a herb garden.

'Bread and cheese for breakfast, and for Penguin a little left-over eel.'

Isadora Elzbeth made a sick face at Penguin, but he seemed to be annoyed at her over something, so she sat quietly and watched Sia move about fetching things from the larder. She listened to her talk and tried to avoid answering her questions.

'After breakfast I will give you some of that ointment I was telling you about. You'll feel better for it. So, your cat's name is Penguin and you come from a place called Dublin. I tried to find it on the map last night, but it must be a very small place because it wasn't marked.'

Isadora Elzbeth tried to deflect the conversation that she felt was coming. 'Where is here?'

Sia turned away from the range she had just lit, and her lake-blue eyes looked towards the window.

'This is Arcadia.' She smiled ironically.

'Arcadia,' Isadora Elzbeth repeated, half-surprised by the word.

'Yes,' Sia confirmed as she sliced some bread. 'My father was greatly amused by the name of this country; that's why he settled here. You see, Arcadia is the Latin word for 'paradise', and it seems everyone wants to live in paradise. I, on the other hand, would like to see Dublin, the place of the flying balloons.'

'Are you a doctor?' Isadora Elzbeth dived in, trying to push the conversation away from herself. Sia shook her head, and offered a slice of bread and herb cheese to Isadora Elzbeth.

'Not really, though I do have some medical knowledge, but it's science that fascinates me. Chemicals. And I also like to dabble in construction design and of course a bit of gardening.' Sia was poised on the edge of another enquiry, she was going to ask about Dublin, or balloons or antiques shops or something, so Isadora Elzbeth raced ahead trying to dodge the artillery of questions that were bound to come her way.

'Chemistry is interesting; it involves chemicals and things.'

Penguin sneered. 'State the obvious, whatever you do.'

Sia poured boiling water into cups through a sieve full of leaves.

'I come from a long line of chemists,' she said. 'My father ended up being a physician, but he started out being a chemist. My grandmother was a metallurgist, and an extremely fine one as well. She drew up a profile table on

122

metals, what she called the Dramatis Personae. You know, that zinc is a galvanising metal, nickel versatile, vanadium one of the scavenging metals, and so on. She was a very fine woman.'

Sia placed the steaming cups on the table, sat down and cut straight to the point.

'So tell me about yourself, Isadora Elzbeth. Tell me who you are, and what Dublin is like?'

The question was so bald that Isadora Elzbeth had to swallow hard and look at her food to hide her panic-stricken face. She took a deep breath, and for the first time in her life lied with intent.

'I don't seem to be able to remember much. I was thinking about all those things this morning, and I remember my name, and that I like moths, and that there was a pear tree in my garden, but that's it. All the other details are blank.'

Sia was obviously disappointed. Her very pale eyes filled with sympathy, and she nodded. 'After a fall like that it's amazing that you can string sentences together and walk! The amnesia will go, I assure you. I'll send for a messenger tell him to bring word to the city that a Fräulein Isadora Elzbeth is safe and well after her recent accident, and is currently residing with Ambrosia Wish. That way your friends will know where to look for you. In the meantime, you can wear one of my little sister's dresses; you'll find them up in her wardrobe in the room you slept in. I've washed your dress. We can work in the garden today.'

A silence fell over the table. Isadora Elzbeth was glad there would be no more questions. She watched Penguin eat the blanched flesh of cooked eel, and she just couldn't bring herself to swallow any more bread and cheese.

Sia went back out to the garden, leaving Isadora Elzbeth a jar of ointment with instructions to rub it in all over. She made her way upstairs to get dressed; the sweet smell of wild roses lingered in the room. Opening the black carved door of the wardrobe she looked into its dark interior. It was empty. There were no dresses hanging up. She pulled out the top drawer beneath the door; it was packed with papers and pencils and boxes of papers and pencils. Papers and pencils everywhere.

'Marianne wrote a lot,' Isadora Elzbeth observed. She found a handmade card, sewn with red ribbon. On the front was drawn a beautiful red apple and inside was written a single question, *Will you be my Valentine?*

'She made a valentine card,' she told Penguin, 'a long, long time ago.' As she replaced it and closed the drawer, she wondered who the card had been for.

When she opened the next drawer, silks and cottons of every description bubbled up. She pulled out a blue-coloured dress; it was long but it looked as if it might fit her. She tried it on. There was no mirror in the room, but she knew she was going to trip over the skirt if she didn't take it up.

'There's something not right about it,' she explained to Penguin, but he let her know in no uncertain terms that he was not talking to her.

'I am not talking to you, I practically sat on your face and pulled your hair, and you didn't wake up last night.'

She opened the third drawer and found lines of little boots. She took out a brown button-up pair and, as she did, she saw beneath them two silver serpents entwined. She thought they moved, and was about to slam the drawer shut when she realised that they were not alive. They weren't eels wriggling in a drawer, they were two silver snakes hammered into the red velvet cover of a book. She pulled the book out from under all the boots, and knew before she opened it that it had belonged to Marianne.

On the first page Marianne had written her name. *Marianne Wish.* And on the second page, she had written, *All that you read here has been sealed, and the secret shall go with me to my grave, for the way of the Alchemist is never to reveal.*

'A book on alchemy,' Isadora Elzbeth thought, but when she turned the pages her heart sank, for she understood none of it; it was all gibberish.

'Penguin, what are we to do? I bet there are so many answers in here. Like how we got here, or maybe the answer to the crow's riddle, or how to get back to our own time, and I can't read it.'

'I told you, I'm not talking to you.'

Isadora Elzbeth closed the drawer and hid the book under her pillow. She put on Marianne's boots, which were surprisingly comfortable. They had a tiny heel, making her feel very grown-up. Holding up the skirt of her dress, she went down to join Sia in the garden.

Sia was weeding the rose patch. 'I was thinking,' she

said, without looking up, 'perhaps we should take you to the city. It would make more sense. I have business there in two days' time, and I'm sure that's where your friends will start looking for you. The blue dress.'

Sia had turned her head and seen Isadora Elzbeth. There was something sore in her voice, and her pale eyes filled up.

'Marianne swore that that blue dress brought her luck. She'd have congratulated you on your choice. You've forgotten to put the frame in. I'll get it for you; you'll trip over yourself otherwise.'

Sia returned with a wire skirt and Isadora Elzbeth tied it around her waist. The blue dress fell round her, fitting perfectly.

'There, pretty as a picture.'

Sia returned to her gardening and worked away quietly, thinking her own thoughts. Isadora Elzbeth watched for a bit. She offered to help, but Sia said softly, 'Not at all. You rest, give yourself a chance to heal.'

Penguin stretched out in a square of scorching sunshine and lay there drinking it in, blinking lazily at the damselflies. The mixture of the warm sunshine and the scents from the garden were comforting. Isadora Elzbeth looked beyond the garden wall at the distant trees and the pointy snow-capped mountains. She expected to see the Darkman, but instead she saw a cowboy riding towards her.

'There's someone coming,' she said.

Sia stood up and shaded her eyes. 'Oh, it's Will. You'll like him, he's a painter. Wait until I tell him that you fell

126

out of the sky. Hello, Will,' Sia called, waving her big arms over her head. The man took off his hat and waved back.

Penguin was sitting on the gate pillar, eagerly awaiting a fellow male specimen.

Will was riding a chestnut stallion. As he drew near there was something very familiar about his form. Sia opened the gate and strode out to meet him. Isadora Elzbeth stayed behind, and she stroked Penguin's back and watched as Will jumped off his horse and kissed Sia's hand. He was tall and slender, with dark spiky hair. He stood and listened while Sia spoke to him, and then he looked at Isadora Elzbeth and began walking towards her with big manly strides. She couldn't believe it. He was thinner, younger maybe, but the man approaching her was, in another life, Johannes Handley. Isadora Elzbeth jumped back. Will stopped and raised his hand.

'I didn't mean to frighten ye. My name is Will.' He walked slowly now, his face flushed, his hawk-green eyes sharply observing.

'Sia tells me ye fell from the cloud storm that passed over yesterday.'

He was Johannes Handley, and yet he was not Johannes Handley. He wore a floppy white shirt, tobacco-coloured trousers and high riding-boots. His cheeks were chiselled, his body was more sinewy, his eyes were brighter, but somewhere there was definitely a connection between Will from the past and Johannes from the future. The words DNA popped out of Isadora Elzbeth's mouth, making Will frown.

'Ye de not ney. Are ye Scottish?'

127

'No, no.' Isadora Elzbeth couldn't help but giggle. Sia was with them now.

'She does not know if she fell out of the cloudburst. Are ye tellin' me lies, Sia?'

Sia shook her large head and raised her eyebrows. 'Now why would I lie to you, Will?'

'To aggravate me,' he quipped. Then turning to Isadora Elzbeth he said, 'She's a beauty, all right. Sia told me ye were a beauty. I'll paint ye, if ye've no objection.'

Isadora Elzbeth couldn't think of any, so she said nothing. Because Will looked so like Johannes Handley she felt like she knew him, and she listened while he spoke to Sia.

'What of her kin?' he asked.

'She was travelling with two others.'

'They'll be looking for ye,' he said to Isadora Elzbeth. 'The mad scientist here told me ye were in a flying machine. Is it true?'

When Isadora Elzbeth nodded, Will groaned with disbelief. 'I was afraid ye'd say that. What's the plan, Sia? Are ye going to try and build a contraption to carry us beyond the mountains?'

Sia shook her head. 'And leave Arcadia behind?' They both laughed, shook their heads in unison and in funny accents said, 'Ya! Who vould vant to leave paradise?'

Isadora Elzbeth didn't really get the joke, so she waited for them to finish laughing before telling Will what the plan was.

'We are going to the city to look for Christina and Marian in a few days. I'll be a bit better by then. This is my cat Penguin.' Then she didn't have anything else to say, and she felt embarrassed about being so familiar with Will. She blushed uncomfortably and remembered the valentine card in Marianne's drawer. The questions suddenly made sense to her. Will you be my Valentine was a question for Will.

'I'll be heading into Arcadia myself on business in two days' time. We can travel together, Sia and myself that is.' He looked seriously at Sia. 'I think it'd be safer for the lass to stay at home, do ye nae agree, Sia?'

But Isadora Elzbeth was having none of it. 'You won't recognise Marian and Christina. Besides, I can't stay here on my own. Anyway I'd like to see Arcadia.'

Will looked preoccupied for a while. 'I suppose ye can not stay here alone,' he reasoned. 'Well, perhaps we can travel together.' He didn't seem so sure, but Penguin was pleased.

He meowed his approval: 'Thrilled to hear it. Do you drink bourbon?'

Will laughed and patted Penguin's head, but he didn't answer the question, instead he removed a book from his saddle bag and left his horse to graze.

They all walked down the garden and sat on a sunny bench. Sia went in to make lemonade and, while she was gone, Will began sketching Isadora Elzbeth and asking her questions.

'Sia tells me ye've lost yer memory.'

'It fell out in the fall,' Isadora Elzbeth said, flustered by the fact that she had to lie. Will laughed a hearty, manly laugh.

'So you've no recollection of anything?'

Isadora Elzbeth shook her head, then, desperate to pull the subject away from herself, she asked what was inscribed on the lintel over the door. Will didn't have to look at it, he knew the inscription by heart and he repeated it in a loud, ceremonious voice, that was hollow and mocking.

The brazen serpent was fastened to the cross, so that they should recover from the plague which they deserved and suffered. Therefore know that if you fasten the serpent Python to this cross with a golden nail, you will lack nothing in wisdom.

Signed: Abraham Eleazar 1735

Will spoke and drew at the same time. Isadora Elzbeth couldn't help but be still; Will's deep-green eyes made her want his respect, and if she was sitting for him he would respect her not moving. Two minutes of silence passed, then Isadora Elzbeth knotted her forehead.

'Aren't you going to explain it to me?'

Will relaxed. He took in a deep breath, looked at the lintel and shrugged his shoulders.

'I'm not too sure that I understand it myself. It's an alchemical prophesy, written by Abraham Eleazar; at least that's the name at the bottom of it. Sia put it there after Marianne died.'

He made the name Marianne sound musical. 'There was a plague in Arcadia, and thousands died. Little Marianne was the last to go. The very last one.' He couldn't say anything else. He lowered his head and began shading Isadora Elzbeth's portrait. She thought it best not to ask him questions about Marianne; neither he nor Sia seemed able to talk about her. Instead she posed, still as stone, while Will drew. When Sia came out with a tray of glasses and a jug of cloudy water, Isadora Elzbeth felt faintly disappointed. She had expected fizzy stuff.

'Lemonade,' Sia announced, smiling her crooked smile. She lowered the tray onto the bench and distributed the glasses. Isadora Elzbeth sipped. It was the most delicious lemonade she had ever tasted. She offered some to Penguin and he licked thirstily from the same glass.

They were sitting happily in the warm sunshine, drinking lemonade, talking about the garden, telling Isadora Elzbeth the names of plants and trees, the names of the districts nearby, and of the snow-capped mountains.

'You fell into Gabriel's Peak. Which of course doesn't make sense, because there's no mountain there.'

Isadora Elzbeth looked in the direction where Sia was pointing, to the circle of larch trees that shielded the strip of marsh land where she had fallen. She remembered the Darkman.

'It's called after the Archangel Gabriel. Some legend about his wandering in the marshes.' Will glugged at his lemonade and went on, 'I've painted him. In the church where I live.'

Isadora Elzbeth held her glass in mid-air, frozen. 'You've seen him, the Darkman? I mean, the Archangel Gabriel?'

Even Sia laughed, but the laugh had a faint tinge of sadness in it. 'Who does she remind you of?' she asked Will, and he nodded, 'especially in that blue dress.'

Isadora Elzbeth felt uncomfortable. She didn't like to remind anybody of anyone, she wanted to be a one and only, not like anybody else. She blinked her big grey eyes and Will drifted back to the point.

'No, lass, I did na' see the Archangel Gabriel, though there's plenty of folks says he roams the foot of The Gate Mountains, keeping watch on the citizens of Arcadia. Stealing a few of them as well, by all accounts. It's all rubbish. I painted him from my head; made him look stern and vengeful. Ye know he is the angel of death? Blows his golden trumpet on judgement day, heralds in the grim reaper.' Will's moss-green eyes darkened over. 'He is the bringer of death, and the bringer of life.' Will leaned back and laughed his story away. 'I am an empiricist, lass. I see what is, and what I do not see, I do not believe. Most of us in Arcadia are so; in fact I'd nearly say all of us think such things. Pragmatists, the lot of us. Are ye religious?'

Isadora Elzbeth didn't know what to answer. A memory of her father and mother flickered inside her head. She thought of the moon and the moths, and Penguin and her singing by the river, and when she answered she surprised herself.

'Yes. I think so.' Then she asked, 'Why do you live in a church?'

'Because it's a wonderful space. It had been left, disused. When I moved in, there was a large hole in the dome letting in the rain and wind. I blocked it over and turned the building into my studio. Ye'll see it on yer way to the city.' He finished off his glass and gathered up his sketchbook. 'Well, I'd better be on my way. What do ye think?' He showed Isadora Elzbeth the portrait he had been working on. She needn't have bothered keeping so still, for he hadn't drawn her sitting on a garden bench in the warm sunshine. Instead he'd drawn her tumbling out of the clouds, her dark hair waving behind her, the circle of The Gate Mountains pointing up at her, and the empty waste of Gabriel's Peak waiting to suck her in. It was a very dramatic, accurate portrait. Isadora Elzbeth wanted to keep it.

'You forgot to put Penguin in, he was clinging to my dress.'

Will took note of this detail and said, 'I'll remember that for the fresco. I'm going through a fresco phase at the moment.' He closed the sketchbook, slipped his pencil into the rim of his hat and looked at Sia.

'Now, the real reason I came to visit, besides, of course, seeking out yer charmin' company. I have somethin' for ye.'

He rooted in his trouser pocket and pulled out a folded sheet of paper. He handed it to Sia, her large hand took it and opened it up. She read it keenly, when she looked up her face had altered.

'Where did you get it?'

Will rose to his feet, and tapped his nose. 'Providence has a curious way of supplying information.'

Sia's flirtatious smile was closed and crooked, she jumped up and her statuesque form was all solid curves.

She pointed to the page. 'You won't leave me hanging on a thread, Will. I want to know where you got this, and are you sure it's correct?'

'Now don't be asking me what I cannot possibly answer. Sure, I wouldn't know moon from copper in its liquid form. Ye'r the expert on metals.'

He looked as if he was about to leave, so Sia reached out and rested her hand on his arm. 'But the recipe is in a mixture of languages, Hebrew, Arabic and Chinese.'

'There, ye see, it all looked the same to me.' Will put his hat on his head and snapped his heels together. He bowed and turned to fetch his horse, saying, 'I found it in a travel log, among the church records. I thought it might help yer current project, looking for the Chinese milk ceramic. It could be nothing, Sia, don't get yer hopes up too high. I thought it was interesting, that's all, thought it might be useful.' He walked into the meadow, and Sia and Isadora Elzbeth followed.

Penguin ran ahead through the long grass, every now and again stopping to say, 'Can I persuade you to stay a while longer? What's the rush? It's not like much happens here?'

Will mounted and, smiling down, said to Isadora Elzbeth, 'It's nice to have new company again. We tend to avoid the city as much as possible, Sia and me. Recluses both.' He looked at Sia and their look lingered, like some silent agreement hanging in the air between them. 'See you in two days' time.' He clasped the harness of the horse and jigged him forward and around. 'Good-day, ladies. I hope ye'll remember everything soon, Isadora Elzbeth, I am anxious to hear of the place where you are from.'

He slapped the rump of his horse with his hat, and galloped off towards the shady larch trees. Sia looked after him with her pale eyes and Isadora Elzbeth felt sorry that both Sia and Marianne had been in love with the same man.

The rest of the day passed in a long lingering heat that made Isadora Elzbeth so lazy she didn't even bother to worry about the future, or about getting back to it. She sprawled out on the bench and asked Sia if she could take off the wire-frame skirt, because it was very uncomfortable. She stroked Penguin, listened to Sia sing while she worked in the garden, and eventually dozed off with the perfume of gardenia wafting over her.

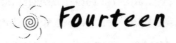# Fourteen

Recipe to Make Sun (Gold)

Take the herb called wild cotton; similar to cotton
Except that its wool is yellow. When you find it
Take its leaves and squeeze out their water, and then
Soak Moon (silver) in it and change the water six times
And behold it will become pure gold. And Seal this.

The Jewish Theological Seminary Manuscript, 16th Century (Folio 11b:A)

*I*t was the cool evening breeze that woke Isadora
Elzbeth. She was alone. Goose bumps pricked her arms.
Where was everybody? She sat up stiffly; a scarf of clouds
wisped over the mountain peaks. She scanned the larch
trees, suddenly afraid of seeing the Darkman. Emptiness.
No one around. She wanted to call out 'hello', but the
silence was so dominating that she couldn't. Instead she
whispered, 'Penguin. Are you there?' Not even a songbird
sang; the only sound was the rustle of the wind in the grass.
Isadora Elzbeth felt her heart icing up, and she began to be
afraid.

'I am in a very strange place,' she reminded herself, 'and I have to get out of it.'

A crow swooped out over the chimney and shrieked Isadora Elzbeth's name. A flutter of black feathers tangled in her hair, a wing brushed her face. She ran away, in through the open door to the hollow emptiness of the hallway. She stood panting, the door half-closed behind her, and peeked out. With one grey eye she saw the crow wheel over the rose garden and fly towards Gabriel's Peak. She watched it flapping its black wings, until it shrank to a speck and finally disappeared out of sight. She opened the door tentatively and looked into the empty sky, where the first star of evening was shining. She knew he would be near it, and he was. When she looked down, the Darkman was standing watching her from across the meadow. He did not move, he just let her see that he was there. For a moment she wondered if he had anything to do with the crow, but she shook this idea out of her head. Stepping backwards, she moved away from the door and into the shade of the hall.

The hallway was filled with honeyed colours and sleepy muteness. The clock tick-tocked dreamily in the corner, one time, one time, one time, one time. For a while she stood mesmerised, watching the pendulum swinging backwards and forwards, until she began to feel drowsy. Suddenly there was an unexpected boom.

'Oh my God!' She jumped. The noise, whatever it was, seemed to come from under the stairs. Another clatter, an iron blow like the strike of a hammer, cut through the air. The noises were definitely coming from under the

137

stairs. Isadora Elzbeth crouched down beneath the steps and there it was, a sunken door. Behind it she heard muffled movement, a hiss of fire, the glug of liquid, a suppressed bubbling noise. Then she heard Sia's voice.

'Oh blast. They've exploded again. Don't go near it, it's scorching hot.'

There was a lot of rummaging and shuffling about. Isadora Elzbeth tapped at the door.

Silence.

She knocked again, a little harder this time, her heart fluttering because somehow she felt she should not be there. The silence was deafening. Confused and uncomfortable, Isadora Elzbeth was about to return to the living-room when an incredulous whisper slipped under the door.

'Marianne?'

What does she mean, Marianne? Marianne is dead, how could I possibly be Marianne? Isadora Elzbeth thought. Didn't they bury her? She didn't know what to do. In the end she decided to ignore the question, to pretend she hadn't heard Sia whisper her sister's name.

'Hello,' she said loudly, 'I'm very sorry to disturb you at your work, but I was wondering if Penguin was with you, only I can't find him anywhere.'

'Oh, Isadora Elzbeth, of course it's you. Can you give me a minute? Penguin is here, all right. Just a moment.'

When Sia opened the door she had Penguin in her arms. Her face was layered with patches of fine, chalky dust, and a sulphurous odour drifted out over her shoulders.

'He's a good cat, excellent company.'

Isadora Elzbeth was only half listening, she was far more curious about the space behind the door. 'Are you trying out the recipe that Will gave you?' she asked boldly.

Sia's long mouth crinkled at the corners; she was smiling her crooked smile. Nodding, she stepped back from the door and silently invited Isadora Elzbeth to follow her into her laboratory.

'Don't touch anything,' she advised. 'Some things may be a bit toxic.' She pointed to a shallow dish where globes of mercury wobbled. 'Quicksilver, for example; deadly poisonous. And there's arsenic over there sweetening by the window. It's got a delicious smell, almondy, but don't think of tasting it. One grain and your system would collapse, it will choke your heart and turn your tongue black.'

The laboratory was a mess, a clutter of vessels and vile smells, and everything was piled on top of each other. The loose innards of some animal were fossilising on an open tray.

'Antelope's liver. Particularly effective for curing "the ague",' Sia remarked, casually tossing the tray aside.

She must have her nose plugged, Isadora Elzbeth thought as her stomach retched at the various rancid, chemical smells. A dead rat hung suspended from its tail on what looked like a washing-line stretched over one of the furnaces. Shelves and shelves of jars filled with brightly coloured liquids preserved everything from roots to chunks of intestine. Lines of wooden drawers stretched around the room; they contained an array of powders and metals.

'Welcome to my Alchemist's Lair,' Sia said, spreading

139

her arms out to include the whole disgusting mess. Isadora Elzbeth tried to smile, but she was shocked. The repulsive odours were making her dizzy, and she felt faint.

'It's extremely hot in here,' she said clutching the table.

'Heat is a necessary agent for transmutation,' Sia said as she stoked up one of the furnaces. 'I mean, to change things you need heat.'

Isadora Elzbeth nodded weakly, she hadn't expected an alchemist's laboratory to be so stuffy. Clustered on the table was a circular knot of live spiders all tangled in their own webs. Beside them there were pots with spouts bubbling on what looked like little candle-lit ovens.

'There is strychnine in the web, it's very good for clotting blood. If you have a cut lay a bit of web over it. It's also good for swollen ankles.' Sia followed Isadora Elzbeth's gaze to three cubes of gold standing in a neat row beside a gold cup. Sia came up beside her, took one of the cubes and looked at it. 'You know the Count of Saint-Germain gave me a recipe. Do you remember my speaking about a very handsome, charming man, with whom I almost fell in love?' Sia's jutting face, with its high cheekbones, long mouth and pale eyes, held a secretive expression.

'The Count of Saint-Germain,' Isadora Elzbeth nodded, 'I remember you talking of him.'

'The man was a genius. He gave me so many recipes, for dyes and things. He has a factory, you know, in Otte at Eckernfoerde, where he can make his beautiful colours. He taught me how to make this.' She held the gold cube so Isadora Elzbeth could see it. 'He taught me how to make gold,' she said, shaking her head and smiling broadly. 'Have you any idea how many men since the beginning of time have searched for the recipe to change base metal into gold?'

Isadora Elzbeth shook her head.

'Countless numbers, all cooped up in their pungent laboratories, locked away from the world, slaving over hot fires, experimenting with metals and chemicals and temperatures. Countless numbers down through the centuries, tragic men and women, some of them misguided scientists with greed burning in their hearts.'

Isadora Elzbeth felt nauseous. She spotted a rancid worm-eaten mouse curled beneath a drinking glass.

'You see many of them only wanted to make gold to become rich.' Sia was absorbed in her speech, oblivious to the fact that Isadora Elzbeth felt she was dying. 'Whereas, the Count of Saint-Germain was a true chemist. He was interested in the process, in the beauty of the "change". He was in love with that moment when one thing transforms into another. That split second when a metal becomes gold. He knew how to make gold by the age of fifteen! Can you believe it?'

Isadora Elzbeth closed her eyes. Don't throw up, she kept telling herself.

'He could have made mountains of gold, and been the richest man in the world,' Sia went on, 'but it was valueless to him. What is gold compared to watching the beauty of one chemical transforming into another? We got on very very well. He could play the violin and sing so beautifully. He saw that I was a keen student of chemistry, with a sound head, so he showed me how to make gold and then he advised me strongly never to produce it. That gold cup and these three cubes are the result of a wonderful afternoon spent working together.'

Isadora Elzbeth opened her eyes. She wanted to say something, but she was afraid of what might come out. Sia put the gold cube into Isadora Elzbeth's hand. 'A talisman for your journey. Something to remember me by.' Sia stirred something inside one of the pots bubbling on the candle-lit ovens and said, 'Shall I tell you something about alchemists?'

Isadora Elzbeth wanted to say, No, please don't talk any more, I'd rather go out and breathe.

'There's a legend about alchemists, about those alchemists who eventually succeeded in their experiments. They say they stay hidden from the rest of the world, because as they become more enlightened they disappear from normal human sight. The most enlightened keep in touch with each other, like a very secret society. They are allowed to have one assistant, an apprentice, to whom they can pass on all their knowledge. Over the last few hundred years there are stories of alchemists suddenly appearing, dark men and women, searching out apprentices and then mysteriously disappearing again, magically, without warning.'

Isadora Elzbeth immediately thought of the Darkman.

Sia chuckled and shook her large head. 'So many stories about alchemy and magic.' Her expression became taut. 'It is a serious business, the pursuit of knowledge, and chemistry in particular can be obscure enough without silly stories clouding the issue. Do you know what I am trying to do?'

she asked, and her face was so intensely alive that Isadora Elzbeth didn't have the heart to say 'tell me tomorrow'.

'Come and look at this.' Sia moved gracefully through staggering piles of wood, past the dangling rat to a large wrought-iron safe. She turned a dial of secret combinations with her ear pressed against the black door before heaving it open. Isadora Elzbeth tried to breathe through her teeth. She stood delicately behind Sia's large back and waited for a treasure chest to be brought out before her. Instead, Sia turned holding a glass dome and beneath the glass there stood what looked like a cup and saucer.

'The greatest conundrum of modern times!' Sia announced and her pale eyes looked lovingly through the glass.

Isadora Elzbeth's heart sank. 'Oh no,' she thought, 'she seemed so sane. I should have guessed it when she thought I was her dead sister Marianne. She can make gold, but she'd rather make pottery, and she thinks it's a big fat secret. She seemed so sensible.'

Sia walked carefully to the table, and slowly uncovered her precious crockery. 'The milk ceramic of the Chinese dynasties. Porcelain. The most beautiful and valuable expression of their civilisation. Look, see how the light pours through it, see how pearly it is.'

She held the cup before a candle flame and the light flowed through its thin shell-like surface.

'Isn't it beautiful?'

Isadora Elzbeth couldn't answer. She remembered the story of Augustus the Second locking John Böttger inside

143

his castle and forcing him to make porcelain. When did we discover how to make porcelain? Isadora Elzbeth asked herself. If only she could remember dates.

'You are looking at the best-kept secret of all time,' Sia said proudly, examining the tiny cup pinched between her fingers. 'This is what I am trying to make. My patron is very anxious that I discover how to make it soon; she's an impatient woman. For ten years I've been trying to make porcelain, with everything from talc to chalk. Will's recipe may be the closest yet, look.'

Sia opened a little black door attached to one of the furnaces. 'You see, it has the same exquisite texture, delicate, opaque, look. It's made from kaolin and feldspar mostly. I had been using alabaster but the quartz is fusing better.'

Isadora Elzbeth crouched down to look inside the makeshift kiln. A blast of heat puffed into her face, and there, lying in a dusty heap, were shards of baked clay. It all looked very unpromising.

'The trouble is, the ware keeps exploding.'

Isadora Elzbeth nodded, but she wasn't listening. Her head was spinning, her stomach was lurching. Sia's voice poured over her head and down to her toes. She looked at her feet, and there flicking about was a silvery lizard with glassy wings. Isadora Elzbeth's mouth curled in disgust; she realised the floor was alive with them. Winged lizards with sucker pods on their webbed feet that enabled them to climb vertically. She glanced under the table; a nest of them were feeding in one corner. One wriggled past her face, and she squealed and teetered backwards. She hadn't expected them to be able to fly.

Sia caught her. 'Salamanders, a by-product of the fire. I tried to get rid of them, even tried to drown a couple, but they took like fish to the water. The river's teeming with them. Your cat's been breaking off their tails.'

Isadora Elzbeth passed out. She woke up on the chaise-longue in the sitting-room. Sia was watching her.

'I have been thinking of the place where you come from, Dublin, the place of the flying machines. There are so many things you do not know.' Sia's pale eyes looked troubled. She seemed to want to speak; she opened her mouth and then her eyes glanced at the picture above the fireplace, and it seemed to stop her from talking.

Isadora Elzbeth sat up. 'The girl in the picture with the orange hair, is it Marianne?'

Sia nodded. 'She's not at all like me, is she? We were very different. Pretty, isn't she?'

Isadora Elzbeth smiled. 'She was an alchemist too?'

'Oh yes.' Sia's long mouth burst into a radiant smile. 'She was so curious. Such curiosity.'

'Did she want to make porcelain as well?' Isadora Elzbeth probed. The question fell hard on Sia, who suddenly looked stricken.

'No,' she answered softly. 'She was the other kind of alchemist.'

'The gold maker?' Isadora Elzbeth breathed softly.

'The philosopher,' Sia responded. 'Marianne and the Count of Saint-Germain were in love with the same thing.

The moment of change, when one thing becomes another. She sought to make the 'philosopher's stone'. The agent of immortality. If she could find it.' Sia's voice quavered; she was becoming emotional. She turned her face away but Isadora Elzbeth could see it was flushed.

'The Count of Saint-Germain could make gold, but he advised never to produce it.' She leaned forward in her chair. Her large compassionate face was bewildered. 'You see,' she explained, 'Marianne and the Count of Saint-Germain thought the same way.' Sia leaned back and wiped her face with her large hands, trying to smooth away her difficult thoughts.

Isadora Elzbeth was in the dark. She fumbled, 'So Marianne believed that, if you could make gold, you should not make gold.'

Sia nodded and added, 'If you could make yourself immortal, you should not make yourself immortal!'

Isadora Elzbeth said, 'Ooh yes,' very slowly, as though she understood, but it all seemed pointless to her. Why would you lock yourself up in a laboratory to discover how to do something and then not do it? Round and round in circles. She looked at the picture of the pretty little girl standing in a rose garden reading a book. She had gold-red hair and twinkling green eyes and Isadora Elzbeth thought, 'Poor thing, she can't be more then fourteen there. To think she spent her time cooped-up in a stinking laboratory trying to discover the secret of immortality, only to die. She's dead. Mouldering in her grave.' The idea of a little girl buried in a box underground, with the rain seeping in under the lid, made Isadora Elzbeth shiver. She thought of her mother and her father, but her heart hardened. She blocked everything out and asked Penguin if he was hungry.

All Penguin had to say was 'Spooky-dooky. Got the creeps, crawling up and down my back. Spook-y-doo-ke-doo.' Isadora Elzbeth translated this into a very specific menu, and was glad that Sia shook off her memories to cook bacon and cabbage for dinner.

Over dinner they talked about Will and Arcadia.

'Will was always eccentric,' Sia said. 'He travelled here when the pass was open. It's been blocked for several years now, an avalanche. Arcadia suited him, so he stayed. He's a fine painter. He painted Marianne's portrait. We have the same patron. He has to paint her portrait, and I have to bring her a progress report. The capital of Arcadia is Arcadia – it's not very inventive, is it? It's quite a beautiful city, though I remember a time when it wasn't.' Sia's long mouth closed and she chewed thoughtfully.

'She's just like a moth,' Isadora Elzbeth thought, 'ugly-beautiful.'

'There will be a festival in the city when we arrive. The festival of the Navigator. There'll be lots to do and lots to see, so you won't be bored. Anyway, my patron is a very fine lady,' Sia smiled wryly, 'at least she thinks she is. There's one thing for sure, no one is ever bored when she's around.'

Twilight fell over the conversation. At bedtime Isadora Elzbeth draped Penguin onto her shoulders.

'I don't want to go,' Penguin protested, 'it's very

upsetting. I didn't like it. I bet you won't wake up again. Bet I could bounce all over your head and you'll snore!'

Isadora Elzbeth didn't understand her whining cat. She snuggled down into bed.

'They haven't come looking for me,' she said, trying to entice Penguin to cuddle up under the blankets. 'Christina and Marian. They might have gone down the other side of The Gate Mountains, and the pass is blocked. Suppose they can't get into Arcadia? Suppose they can't find me? Suppose I never return? No one would really miss me, now that . . .' She couldn't say now that Mam and Dad have gone. She bit back the tears and turned over. Penguin slinked over to the window and blinked coolly at the night. He saw a shadow beyond the garden wall. He listened to the soft 'pahh' of Isadora Elzbeth's sleeping breath and he waited.

Deep into the night, long after Sia had gone to bed, and long after the candle had gone out, Penguin heard it: the low whine of a creaking hinge. The door of the wardrobe opened a fraction, just enough to listen by. Penguin waited, his amber eyes fixed with concentration. Four delicate fingers, the colour of moonlight, curled around the edge of the door. A mound of orange-gold curly hair appeared, followed by a girl's face, pale and brilliant as candlelight. She had large mint-green eyes, and pale pink lips. Silently, a foot descended onto the floor, and there was a silky rustle followed by the sweet fragrance of wild roses. The ghost girl was beautiful. Everything about her was translucent, from her blue-white skin to the liquid colour

148

of her inquisitive eyes. Slowly she drifted towards the bed. She stood over Isadora Elzbeth and watched her breathe.

'At last, you have come.' Her tiny voice was like a broken reed. Isadora Elzbeth snorted in her sleep. The ghost girl was troubled. ' You must undo what I have done.' Her voice wavered, faltering like a bad radio reception. She shook her golden hair, and her liquid eyes were forlorn and disappointed. 'Ca . . . ot . . . he . . . r . . . me. Wake up,' she whispered. She reached out her moony hand and tried, ever so gently, to touch Isadora Elzbeth's face. Penguin had had enough.

'Go away!' he howled and Isadora Elzbeth woke up.

'What was that?' she whispered into the darkness. 'I heard the sound of a bell.'

'It was a ghost,' Penguin explained. 'She came out of the wardrobe; she was trying to steal your soul while you slept.'

'Doesn't the room smell nice? Smells of roses.' Isadora Elzbeth sat up and felt along the bed until she bumped into Penguin. 'Come to bed, furry animal, it's the dead of night.'

'That's what I am trying to tell you.'

'And we need our sleep.' Isadora Elzbeth kissed him in the dark, stuffed him under the blankets, and pulled his two front paws out so he looked like a toy in a pram. It was lucky she couldn't see his face, because he was baring his teeth with annoyance. She could hear him growling, but she chose to believe he was purring.

'Night night, catakins. Do you know,' she added

sleepily, 'I feel like there is something I must undo. I was dreaming of a ship and a palace. There was me and you and a beautiful galleon with one hundred sails. And the most beautiful of starry nights.' Her voice trailed off. 'I love the smell of roses. Remind me there is something I must undo.' She breathed deeply and while she slept Penguin kept a beady eye on the wardrobe door.

⚙ Fifteen

For Pearl, that they should become white.
Take trementina (turpentine) and salt in equal parts,
In al-anbiqi (alembic) in mild fire, and something like oil will come
out of them. If you put the pearl into this oil for the time required
to count a hundred for the most, it will become white.

The Jewish Theological Seminary Manuscript, 16th Century

'*Is she goin' to sleep the day long ?*'

Isadora Elzbeth rolled over and opened her eyes. Will
and Sia were smiling down at her.

'I was just askin' if ye were goin' to sleep the long day?'
Will poked her ribs and pointed to the daylight bursting
through the window.

'What time is it?' Isadora Elzbeth sat up and blinked
her dreams away.

'It's time ye were up and about. A young lass like you
should be up with the sun in the mornin'. Shouldn't she, Sia?'

Sia shook her head. 'Don't mind Will. It's still very
early. We were thinking, why put off until tomorrow what
can be done today? I told Will you were feeling much

better, so we thought we'd go to the city today, to see if we can find your friends.'

Isadora Elzbeth bounded out of bed. 'That's great,' she said. 'Today, Arcadia today,' and Will and Sia laughed at her enthusiasm.

'I take credit for the idea,' Will said, slipping an arm around Sia's shoulder and guiding her out of the room. 'Hurry up and get dressed. Breakfast is ready. That cat of yours is downstairs muttering into his fish pie. He meows a lot, doesn't he?'

Isadora Elzbeth nodded and waited for the door to close before slipping into Marianne's blue dress and brown button-up boots.

Breakfast was a rushed, giddy affair. Will was good-humoured, Sia was flirtatious, and Penguin was glad there was a man about. The table buzzed with conversation.

'We'll be passin' my place, it's en route. Ye can take a look at the fresco I did of ye last night.'

'You've done a fresco already?' Isadora Elzbeth's eyes flung wide open with admiration – if only she knew what a fresco was. Will laughed.

'At last a girl who appreciates my dedication and diligence. Someone who admires me, not only because I'm handsome, but because I'm a swift painter!'

Isadora Elzbeth noticed that Sia blushed, but she could only laugh at Will. 'I wouldn't be too confident,' she said, slapping him down gleefully, 'I haven't seen it yet. You might be a terrible quick painter.'

Will chuckled into his tea. 'Ye've a bright wit. We'll

see how long it lasts in Arcadia. Ye've yet to meet our patron. Will we warn her, Sia, or shall we let her discover all on her own?'

Isadora Elzbeth groaned. 'That's not fair. If there is something I should know, you should tell me.'

Will smiled smugly. 'I dennae know. It could be fun watching your reaction to her Majesty. It'd be nice to see how ye think on yer feet.'

'She's a queen?' Isadora Elzbeth dropped her spoon into her fruit salad, but all that greeted her question was an explosion of laughter from Sia and Will.

'She thinks she's a queen,' Sia said, 'but no, she's not a queen. She's retired.'

Isadora Elzbeth looked into Sia's pale-blue eyes. 'Retired from what?' she asked.

Before Sia could answer, Will interrupted. 'Now do not tell her, Sia darlin'. The lass will get it within three guesses, I guarantee it. You're a clever slip of a thing. Let's see if ye can guess which profession our patron had. It'll be a game. If ye guess correctly, I'll reward ye with a present.'

Isadora Elzbeth felt excited. She wanted to meet Will and Sia's patron straight away so she could show Will just how clever she was.

'What's her name?' Isadora Elzbeth asked, but Will raised his hand to stop Sia saying it. 'Tell her nothing. The lass gets no clues. After all, we dennae know how wide our patron's reputation is. She were very famous before her retirement, and that's all I'll say. Have ye not finished eating yet?'

Isadora Elzbeth scooped up large chunks of syrupy fruit. She was eager to begin her journey home.

'There,' she said through her last mouthful, 'finished.'

Will rose and put on his jacket. He was dressed in corn-coloured trousers today with a smart waistcoat to match. His shirt was sparkling white, and when he put his dark riding jacket on he looked clean and handsome. He reached for his hat and told Sia he was going to fetch the horses. They had both taken time over their appearances. Sia had bound up her hair in intricate plaits that pulled away from her face, accentuating her fresh skin and long elegant neck. She was wearing a burgundy dress that made Isadora Elzbeth think of a bottle of wine.

'I'll get the wire frame for your skirt,' Sia said, and Isadora Elzbeth didn't have the heart to protest. She politely put it on and waited out in the garden while Sia locked up. It was only when Will came riding round the corner of the house, with two extra horses trotting behind, that she realised they expected her to ride a horse. What was she going to do? She'd never ridden a horse in her life. What was she going to say? 'We have cars back in Dublin!'

She panicked quietly. 'Everyone must have known how to ride in the eighteenth century. What am I going to do?'

Will jumped down off his brown stallion and, before Isadora Elzbeth could say 'broken neck', he had swung her up into the air and onto the back of a dappled grey. She wobbled and grabbed, clutching the horse's mane, steadying herself enough to say, 'Thank you very much.' There

154

were numerous things wrong, besides the obvious fact that she didn't know how to ride a horse. Firstly, her skirt was bunched in a strange ball above her knees, secondly, she was sliding down one side, and when the horse dipped his head to munch the grass she nearly tumbled down over its ears. Thirdly, the horse was all out of proportion; he was far too tall, she was far too high up off the ground. She wanted to ask lots of questions, like, 'Don't you have a miniature one of these? A Shetland pony maybe? Something stubby, more my height? How do you start the thing? Do you expect me to gallop?'

Sia shut the garden gate behind her and stuffed a pile of journals and packages into her saddlebags. Will and she had a mini-conference. Isadora Elzbeth heard the word 'danger', but she was too busy being terrified of her horse to think that things could get any more dangerous.

Will picked Penguin up and handed him to Isadora Elzbeth. 'Here, lass.'

She stuffed him onto her shoulders while Penguin hissed, 'Judas.'

'Now,' Will instructed, shoving his wide-brimmed black hat onto his head, 'don't let the beast get the better of ye. Hold the reins tight. Are ye not goin' to use the stirrups?' A shadow passed over his twinkling eyes. 'Ye have ridden before?'

Isadora Elzbeth nodded. 'It has been a long time.' She was going to say, 'I'm sure it's like riding a bicycle, you never forget,' but she couldn't remember when the bicycle was invented, so she let that saying lie.

'You never forget!' Will said, bounding up onto his horse. Without a backward glance, he smacked the horse's rump and trotted forward. Sia followed and Isadora Elzbeth, desperate not to be caught out, dug one heel into her horse's belly. It jerked forwards and she jerked backwards. Instinctively she gripped its girth with her legs and clenched the reins in her hands. Despite this she was bounced along very uncomfortably. It was awful. Her bones were mercilessly shaken, and Penguin was hanging off her back like a spitting knapsack.

The trot developed into a canter, which was even worse. Isadora Elzbeth was slammed up and down and rocked from side to side, with Penguin clawing at her hair and screeching into her ear.

They travelled like this for miles, across meadows dusted with buttercups, past copses, along clear babbling streams and eventually over a tiny wooden bridge and up a slender avenue lined with feathery cypress trees. If Isadora Elzbeth hadn't been in such pain she would have enjoyed the view. Sia and Will were far ahead, and they eventually disappeared around a corner. By the time Isadora Elzbeth caught up with them, they were nowhere to be seen.

The corner opened up onto a wide circular lawn and, planted dead in the centre, was a small white-domed chapel. A stone angel stood high against the sky. It had startling wings that glistened with mica and curved in two crescents behind its back.

'How do you stop this thing?' Isadora Elzbeth asked, pulling hopelessly on the reins. There was only one thing for it. She flung herself off the trotting horse onto the soft cushioned lawn and rolled to a full stop at Will's feet.

'Ye've an unusual way of dismountin',' Will said, helping her up. 'I don't know if that style will catch on in the city. Ladies flingin' themselves against walls and down steps, there could be damage done, but I suppose there's a knack to it!' His eyebrows rose humorously. 'I did know one man who perfected the skill of somersaulting off his horse, until he cracked his head and died. But ye ladies, ye adopt the most unusual fashions!'

Isadora Elzbeth looked down at the crushed frame of her wire skirt, 'It's been a while,' she muttered apologetically, 'I've forgotten . . .'

'Aye,' Will interrupted, 'ye've forgotten the basics.' And ruffling her hair affectionately, he swept his hat through the air and pointed to the walls behind him.

'Welcome to my humble abode. This is Gabriel's Church; it's more a chapel than a church. Nae longer used as a house of prayer. Come on inside, Sia is preparing a picnic for the journey.' Isadora Elzbeth followed Will stiffly; she had a pain in her left shoulder.

The chapel's cool interior gleamed with smooth elegance. Everything shimmered, the mosaics on the floor, the white marble statues, the gold-domed ceiling supported by a circle of ionic columns.

'It's beautiful,' Isadora Elzbeth whispered.

'Aye,' Will agreed. She followed him to the centre of the chapel, her eyes drawn to the fine details – the carved frieze beneath the dome, the gold baptismal font, the mosaic angels flying across the floor. She spun around to take it all in, then stopped in mid-spin to look at the beautiful extension of the choir.

'Oh,' she exclaimed, surprised by the light.

'My studio space,' Will proclaimed, and Isadora Elzbeth walked towards it.

The choir was bathed in a golden-white light that streamed in from curved windows high overhead. Three easels stood where the altar had once been.

Painted canvases were stacked to one side, but it was the sixty-foot wall that rose behind the easels that took Isadora Elzbeth's breath away. A huge richly painted fresco filled it. Peacock blues, velvety purples, emerald greens, ochres, reverberating reds, poured down from the roof to the floor. Deep, sonorous colours in a picture that told a story. Isadora Elzbeth could see that. Will had painted a walled town, high on a hilltop, crammed with buildings that were sumptuously white and topped with fantastic towers and domes. Behind the town there was a circle of snow-capped mountains, and around it stretched woodlands and fields and thin chalky roads that wound like grey ribbons up to the town gate. There were beggars in the fields, and ragged children at a well, and in the foreground there were three people she recognised, Will, Sia and Marianne, all on horseback. When she looked closer, she realised there was a distant graveyard and bodies piled high on a cart. A crescent moon dangled in the evening sky and, beneath it, just where she expected to find him, she saw the silhouette of a man painted in the shadow of an abandoned church. She knew the story. She saw the ravages of the plague, but still she had to ask Will.

'What does it mean?'

'Ach! It's a memory lass, nothing important now, a time before everything changed, that's all. But see, I've included you.'

He pointed up into the corner furthest away from the moon, ahead of the oncoming starlight. There, tumbling through a rip in the cloud, was Isadora Elzbeth, her dark hair rippling, her red dress billowing up, and Penguin clutching fiercely to one corner.

'I put ye in a scarlet gown, ye strange little airborne lass. Ye almost look as if ye'r flyin'. De ye like it?'

'It's brilliant,' Isadora Elzbeth admitted. 'Is that Arcadia?'

'Aye, but it's the new Arcadia; the old one was ripped down after the plague. I didn't have the heart to paint it as it used to be.'

'The plague?' Isadora Elzbeth queried, but Will went vague.

'Ach, don't bother yer head about it. It's long ago now, ye've nae fear of catchin' it.'

Sia appeared with a basket. 'All packed,' she said. 'Let's go.'

They spilled out into the sunshine, ready to resume their journey, but Penguin was missing. They found him trying to stuff himself inside the cracked base of a pillar.

'Ye'll nae get out of it that way,' Will said, coaxing him out. 'Ye'll come in front, lad, and the lass will sit behind.

The journey will not be so bad after all.'

Will mounted his chestnut stallion, hoisted Isadora Elzbeth up behind him and settled Penguin in the front. Sia watched the proceedings, smiling her crooked smile. She looked like a Celtic warrior queen on her large mare, her curvaceous figure sitting straight, and her burgundy dress draped in folds down over her boots.

She's very dramatic, Isadora Elzbeth thought, and just at that moment Sia's horse bolted. Will's horse followed, and suddenly they were galloping down the avenue with its feathery cypress trees, out over the fields towards woodlands. Isadora Elzbeth clung tightly, her arms wrapped around Will, the world flying by her, the rush of the wind brushing her face. She found herself laughing and, when Will whooped and hollered, she joined in. A galloping horse was exhilarating, much better fun than falling out of a balloon! The hooves pounded, the sky filled with the noise, and the fields fell away as they climbed through woodland up over hills and on towards The Gate Mountains. They rode at speed for what seemed like hours, until finally Sia guided her swift mare out of the woods towards a square of sun-drenched meadow, drawing to a halt near a stream.

'I'll tell ye,' Will said breathlessly as they drew up beside her, 'ye've a skill on the beasts that I have yet to see matched.' Sia coloured under the compliment. She jumped to the ground and unpacked the picnic.

They ate bread and cheese and drank elderflower fizz; they chatted about the Festival of the Navigator and

160

Isadora Elzbeth got excited about all the parades and dances and fireworks and concerts that were promised.

Sia elaborated. 'It's a seafaring pageant. It goes on for a whole week. The theme is nautical, anything to do with sailing or the sea. You should see what people wear! Wigs with tiny ships caught in the piled-up hair, sailor's costumes, nets, sails – which reminds me, I brought your dress. It's got a maritime feel to it, and I found this for you to wear.'

She passed over a green mask, trimmed with bright feathers and tiny coiling seashells.

'You wear it across your eyes,' Sia explained, and Isadora Elzbeth noticed a strange look pass between her and Will.

'Our patron will be fine; she'll not pay ye a shred of attention,' Will said, picking up the thread of a conversation that seemed to be planned between them, 'but ye'r a stranger to these parts, Isadora Elzbeth, and ye'll need protection from prying eyes. It's hard to explain to a little girl, but folk here are greatly curious about travellers. They can be a little over-interested at times. A little zealous.'

He looked under his eyebrows at Sia, and in that look they shared some kind of secret. Sia continued where Will left off.

'It's only a precaution,' she said softly, 'there was no point in worrying you earlier. The people of Arcadia are . . .' she paused, and in the afternoon light her pale eyes darkened. 'The people of Arcadia are foolish and vain. They like baubles and shiny things, and a bright little elfin like you could entertain them for months. Now don't be afraid, but to blend in I think, we think,' she said including Will, 'we think you should put on your green gown and wear the mask. That way you'll look like one of the orphans from St. Paul's and no one will pay any heed to you.'

The whole arrangement was very odd. Isadora Elzbeth sat among the buttercups, pulling beads of long grass through her fingers, trying to figure out why she should blend in. The wind tugged at wisps of her dark hair. She could smell clover and cow-parsley and, when she looked up, her smoky-grey eyes couldn't hide her confusion.

'But I thought the whole point of me going to the city was to attract attention, so that my friends can find me.'

She couldn't help but feel that they were not telling her the whole truth. Will pinched the bridge of his nose and his ruddy face clenched with concentration.

'It's complicated, lass. Believe me, we'll nae have trouble locating yer friends should they be in Arcadia. I'll guarantee they'll be the celebration of the town; we'll have to beat people aside to get at them. The problem will be smugglin' ye out, all of ye.'

Isadora Elzbeth couldn't understand the problem. What were they talking about? Sia shook her large head, and reached out her long arm and brushed a strand of hair away from Isadora Elzbeth's face.

'Don't worry, we'll get you home, all of you. Will and I have a plan. We'll get you out.'

And Will made a lame joke that Isadora Elzbeth didn't understand. In a heavy foreign accent he yelled, 'Ya! who

162

vould vant to leave paradise?' Then, shaking his head, he said, 'Never mind. Now you listen to me, fairy brae, dennae trouble yer head with worryin'. There's naught to fear. Go and put yer mask and gown on; we're aiming to make town by twilight. Our patron is waiting for a string of whitened pearls, and we'll nae be late for such a formidable woman.'

Isadora Elzbeth did as she was bid and put the green gown on, remembering how excited she had felt getting into it at 30 Wexford Street. Now her hands trembled slightly. She was afraid of some unnamed danger that lay lurking in Arcadia. Why were Will and Sia so secretive? What were they hiding? Did they know that she was from another time? Could they have guessed? She stepped out from behind the horse, dressed in her green dress with its lime-lozenge bodice, only to find Will and Sia waiting for her, wearing eye masks of their own, masks that had tiny compasses and clocks and seaweed curls glued to them, and though Isadora Elzbeth smiled, she was a little afraid.

✺ Sixteen

To Remove Hair so that It Should Not Return

Take green frogs called *raqno* (I. or S. *rana*),
Three of them, and put them into a bowl in which
There should be good wine, and let it stand, in the sun
Two months, that is Yulio (July) Agusto (August), and then
Wash your face or the roots of the hair, and it will be
Removed and not to return again.

The Gaster Manuscript (Folio 128b)

The rest of the journey was heavy-hearted. They rode without stopping until the sun was dissolving in red clouds over The Gate Mountains. The first star of evening popped into the purple sky and Isadora Elzbeth rested her face against Will's back, wondering what the dangers of Arcadia were. They stopped on a dusty road skirting a ring of low hills. A mist rose out of the fields, hanging like threads of candyfloss over the grass.

'Two more leagues,' Sia said. 'The twilight will help us.' Her flushed face was quietly animated. She looked deep into Will's eyes and, though he laughed, his laugh rang hollow.

'We'll terrify the lass with all this cloak-and-dagger stuff. Ye'r a bright thing,' he said to Isadora Elzbeth, patting her hand, 'ye can think on yer feet. There's naught to fear, though if you could try not to look so extraordinary it would help!'

He laughed where there was no joke. Sia didn't return his smile. She jigged her horse on and began the last leg of the journey to the city at an easy pace.

The sky was darkening now, deepening into navy, speckled with planets and stars. As Isadora Elzbeth looked at the world through the oval eye-holes of her mask, she noticed a dull star hanging beside the crescent moon. It had a tail of orange and its light was a smear of burnished dust, less vibrant than the usual constellations.

It's like a tadpole, Isadora Elzbeth thought. She had never seen a comet before, and though she knew what it was, she had thought that comets whizzed by the earth in a hail of bright gold light, discharging asteroids, like cinder sparks, in their wake. She didn't expect the comet to just hang there, but that's what it did. It hung like a slipped star, a wet firework, motionless above the peaks of The Gate Mountains.

Arcadia was a shock of white in the dark. They stopped at the sight of it. Isadora Elzbeth's heart fluttered. It was just as Will had painted it, only more brilliant. Every building glistened like ice, every dome glowed with patterned tiles, lanterns hung in long loops over the city walls, and music and laughter filtered down the hillside. It was a spectacular sight and Isadora Elzbeth said so.

'Aye, it is,' Will agreed, but he didn't sound like he meant it. 'It's fortuitous that it's carnival week,' he said, clicking at his horse to ride on.

They approached the city gates at walking pace, giving Isadora Elzbeth all the time she needed to absorb the atmosphere. The castellated walls were the colour of Sahara sand, at least that's what she told herself, and the smooth white buildings looked like they were chiselled out of Carrara marble. The domes sparkled as if they were made from caramelised sugar, and she imagined herself sitting on top of one, mindlessly peeling off one tile after another and eating it. As they drew near the gates she heard music; trumpets and tambourines mixed with laughter. Her curiosity overcame her doubts and she craned her neck for her first glimpse of an Arcadian.

At last they passed under the city gates into the wild carnival. Noise blasted around them. Arcadia's streets were seething with bodies gyrating to the sound of shrill trumpets and pulsating drums. A sea of masked faces and swirling gowns, interspersed with flashes of turquoise and Persian-blue cloaks, fluttered as the people danced. So many people. Isadora Elzbeth suddenly became worried.

The crowd closed in, pressing against the horse's flanks. She hadn't expected this. Braceleted girls climbed up Will's legs and kissed his face. A group tried to drag Sia down to dance. Isadora Elzbeth saw men spilling wine into each other's mouths. She saw children kicking their legs and dancing in rings, and women laughing maniacally, their faces half-hidden, their mouths smeared with fuchsia lipstick. Ratta-tatta-pam! Drums, trumpets, church bells pealing, a screeching, twirling pandemonium. Isadora Elzbeth's heart was bursting; she could feel hysteria frothing beneath the intoxicated frenzy of the crowd. Sia was no longer in sight, Will was being kissed by more and more women, and Penguin was scratching at people's faces. An old woman with whiskey on her breath grabbed Isadora Elzbeth and kissed her full on the mouth, screaming 'Happy holiday, happy Navigator day. Come and dance with old Mogie, come and dance little one.' She had to squirm free of the old hag's bloodless grip. The old woman's sour face sank down into the colourful mass of wigs and silks and whirling bodies. The crowd were maliciously hell-bent on having fun. The drums beat faster, feet thumped, and women revolved round and round and collapsed on top of one another, their dresses knotting up, their shrill laughter piercing through the noise of the music. Men threw punches and pushed each other gruffly.

Startled, Isadora Elzbeth shouted into Will's ear, 'We have to get out of here. Where's Sia?'

Will did his best, but the progress was slow. His horse waded through the revellers until eventually, after what seemed like half an hour of beating people off, they came to an opening in the dancers. Will took advantage of the opportunity and directed his horse down one of the quiet sidestreets, out of harm's way. Isadora Elzbeth looked back at the broiling mayhem. She was glad to be out of the thick of it, and she wrapped her arms around Will as he silently brought the horse through the alleyways and sidestreets.

The streets were claustrophobically narrow, lined with tall houses which, although beautiful, with ornate lintels and doorways, were strangely gloomy as well. The foundations sank in places, buckling the walls. Dark leaden windows frowned down into gutters where wine-stained water flowed in rills. A door was flung open and a woman dressed in fish scales and ribbons ran squealing towards the carnival, followed by two men and a yapping dog.

'Sia will have gone ahead to the villa,' Will said as they rode past a kissing couple pressed up against a wall. 'Arcadia is deceptive, it's not a completely walled town.'

Isadora Elzbeth could feel they were climbing. The narrow streets ran down behind her, and carnival-clad people kept popping out of nowhere, some taunting them as they passed by. One man in particular wouldn't stop shouting, 'The party is that way, you're going the wrong way.'

'Fool,' Will muttered under his breath, but he shouted out, 'Happy holiday, happy Navigator day!'

The horse clip-clopped its way up and up, until finally they reached the crest. Will was right, Arcadia wasn't a small encircled town; it sprawled down over the back of the hillside. There must have been thousands of houses squashed into narrow streets that spread out for miles. Isadora Elzbeth heard music spilling in from all directions, and she saw countless bonfires blazing.

'I'll try to avoid the crowds,' Will told her. 'The villa is to the south. There, do ye see that dark patch with the lit-up building inside it? That is the villa. It's surrounded by beautiful gardens. She has channelled the river into a man-made lake. Rumour has it she plans to perform an opera on it. God help us, the woman thinks she's musical.'

'Who?' Isadora Elzbeth asked, but Will pinched her leg playfully.

'Aha! ye'll nae trick me. Ye guess her profession and I'll tell ye what she's called!'

The gates to the villa were guarded by a hulk of a man wearing a Pinocchio-nosed mask and a harlequin costume. He wore a sword, carried a staff and had a big attitude to match his bulk.

'Your invitation?' he snarled.

'Ah,' Will began in his charming voice, 'our invitations. Here we are.' He passed a silver card into the guard's enormous hand.

'Ya!' the guard nodded officiously. 'This is your invitation, but I do not see the little girl or the cat; they are not mentioned here anywhere. You may pass, but the urchin and the scruffy animal cannot.'

Will's shoulders tensed. He dipped into his pocket and Isadora Elzbeth heard the rattle of gold coins.

'My good man, ye are most diligent to notice such a mistake, but the countess herself wishes to see the girl. This little urchin is a most gifted singer, an orphan from St. Paul's . . .' The guard yawned rudely, but Will talked on. 'The countess only discovered the girl's talent in the last week, and she wishes her to sing a duet in her opera.'

'I heard nothing of the orphan,' the guard barked. 'Now, we can do this the easy way or the hard way.' His

169

large shoulders were squaring up, both hands were clenched around the staff, and his hard mouth began curling up at the edges.

'Oh, my good man,' Will began in mock offence, and then his boot landed with a sharp thud on the guard's face. Before Isadora Elzbeth could squeak, Will was off his horse and punching the guard, until his enormous harlequin body slumped in a heap against the gate.

Penguin made little paw punches on Isadora Elzbeth's lap. 'That's it, jab, jab, wallop. Nice hook with the left. Pamm! Followed by a rock-hard right, pamm! pamm! tjah!'

Will smoothed down his ruffled clothes, gathered up his hat, adjusted his mask and pushed open one of the gates.

'I don't mind a disagreement,' he said smiling, 'it's just I cannae believe I had to fight my way into this ludicrous place.' He lifted Isadora Elzbeth down off the horse. 'We can walk the rest of the way'.

They held hands, Isadora Elzbeth enjoying the jaunty, self-satisfied humour Will was in.

'I hope I dennae have to prove my manliness again when we get to the door. No doubt, if I have to, I could beat ten men to a pulp. Do ye not think so, Penguin?'

'I'd pay to see you do it. Magnificent technique, all that weight behind the right, marvellous stuff.'

'Penguin hopes you won't have to fight again,' Isadora Elzbeth interpreted. She squeezed Will's hand and listened to their boots crunching along the gravel path. The long avenue was lined with triangular-shaped trees and box hedges carved into cubes. In the distance the austere granite villa loomed large against the dark sky. Every mullioned window was lit, and the doorway was ablaze with torches. Despite this fact, the place seemed deserted.

'She's here,' Will said, pointing to Sia's horse grazing on the beautifully manicured lawns. Isadora Elzbeth turned and she saw the Darkman in the shade of the cedar tree, his jet-black eyes watching her walk hand in hand with Will. Up the steps and into the brightly-lit villa they went, out of the darkness and into the white light of a sumptuous hall, with marbled floors, scrolls of carved wood and stone, gilded mirrors, glistening candelabra, and swooping staircases. Everything was glittery and shiny and dripping with wealth.

'It's a palace,' Isadora Elzbeth said, following Will through doors, past paintings and embroidered chairs.

'Ill-gotten gains,' Will snorted.

Chests and statues, Chinese vases, glassware, every imaginable exotic curiosity littered the corridors and spilled out of the deep-carpeted rooms.

'They'll be in the music room,' Will said, checking his reflection in the mirror. He smoothed down Isadora Elzbeth's hair and spoke worriedly. 'Your wild locks will be a fascination. Have ye a kerchief, lass?'

Isadora Elzbeth shook her head, and gasped when Will ripped a cushion open and began wrapping her hair into the material that had once been a cushion cover. She looked ridiculous, but Will seemed satisfied.

'There,' he said smartly, 'yer hair will nae be remarked upon now.'

Before she could say, 'I look stupid,' Will had pulled open two large doors. The swell of violin music surged outwards. Isadora Elzbeth followed him into a grand oval-shaped room crammed with people. Some heads turned, but most remained stiffly poised. Intimidated by the intense atmosphere, she found herself clutching at Will's coat and tiptoeing noiselessly behind him. The air was sickly-sweet with perfume. Ladies decked out in jewels and brightly-coloured silks sat perched on slender chairs to one side of the room, the men on the other. The music was swirling towards a crescendo. Sia was at the back, her large elegant figure a head above the rest of the women in the room. Everyone wore masks, every lady carried a fan, every man carried a lace hanky and a silver box of snuff. Will edged his way down the room to stand near Sia, whose clear skin and sculpted face gleamed with a natural beauty above all the painted ladies around her. She held out her large hand, and Isadora Elzbeth curled onto her lap and snuggled close, listening to the sweet notes that washed over the powdered wigs of the audience.

Everything was going along fine, the music had resolved itself and was digressing into another movement, when a little man in a gold jacket and purple stockings sat down before a harpsichord. He began tinkling the notes and swaying from side to side, his eyes closed in rapture. He had a wizened face and a hooked nose that practically met his chin. Throughout his opening sequence he sucked on his gums and deflated his cheeks. He was making an excellent job of the delicate music when a lady stood up and barged her way through the audience, slapping her fan on heads if people didn't move fast enough.

'Yes, yes, out of the way.' Her heavily accented whisper carried over the music. The little man opened his eyes. He kept playing, but his face was terror-stricken. His fingers rippled over the keys, speeding up in horror as the robust woman charged towards him. She waved her fan at the violinists to keep playing, and then she hit the little man mercilessly about the shoulders.

'Vivace, allegro, largo? Which is it, eh?'

The little man tried to shield his face from her lethal fan, cowering behind one hand while playing with the other.

'Play, play!' the fat woman commanded, her large backside bobbing up and down as she noisily tapped her foot to the music. 'One time, two time, one time, two time.'

Her wide back and muscular arms couldn't be disguised by all the silks she wore. She was a hefty woman, with hips that absolutely did not need accentuating. Her mound of red hair was piled up ridiculously high and was topped with a little lace mantel. Dangling from her fleshy earlobes were clusters of green stones, and clasped around the folds of her neck was a matching necklace. Her huge bovine figure swayed gracelessly and beat out a fierce tempo, until she finally exploded in fury and kicked the little man off his stool.

173

'Out, out out!' she shrieked, and the wizened little man scurried tearfully into the arms of a soldier.

'Like this, you damned imbecile. What are you stopping for?' she roared at the other musicians. 'Play, play, play!' And the Countess Blythe Castiglione sat down at the harpsichord, pounding out Bach with a vicious sense of rhythm that would have had the composer spinning in his grave.

'It's the countess,' Isadora Elzbeth gasped, sitting forward to check the fleshy features she'd seen in a portrait at 30 Wexford Street. She was absolutely certain. It was the Countess Blythe Castiglione, the same fat bossy woman with the loud voice and thick accent that Mrs. Buck had dreamed about!

'Like this, you fool. See? Largo, largo,' she bellowed over the music.

The wizened little man nodded his shrunken head, tears beading up in his eyes.

'Well, come and do it then! Let me see.'

The countess jumped up, leaving the harpsichord to the petrified musician. She stamped down the hall, tut-tutting loudly, and then, in her enormous perfectly audible whisper, she commanded, 'Will! Ambrosia! Meet me in the reception room.'

She plunged past grand ladies and swept noisily out of the music room, leaving the musicians visibly sighing with relief. Sia and Will excused themselves as they passed through the crowd. Isadora Elzbeth draped Penguin over her shoulders and followed.

Sitting on a brocade chair, surrounded by ladies-in-waiting, and stuffing her face with grapes and cheese, Blythe Castiglione bellowed out as Will walked through the door. 'Ya, Will, you were late. It is a good job you are handsome, eh? I forgive only handsome men.' She arched her fleshy body coquettishly. 'Kiss my face, you glorious devil.'

Will kissed her hand, then her elbow, then her neck and finally her plump mouth. An ear-splitting peal of laughter shot around the room.

'You fabulous rogue. Oh I adore you. Ya, Sia, you are here at last. You have brought my whitened pearls? Ya, good. Now, Will, you will excuse us for a fraction of a moment. Sia, come here.'

Blythe beckoned with her chubby hands. She swept her servants away and Will politely stepped back to give both women their privacy. Isadora Elzbeth stood silently observing as Sia gracefully stooped over the large countess. Blythe need not have asked for privacy. She raised her fan to her face and whispered loud enough for everyone in the room to hear, 'Ya, you have found a way of removing the hair on my face. I want to be rid of my moustache for good, but I am sick of bleaching.'

Seventeen

To Make Hair Black

Take fig leaves and burn them and
make of them a lisia (solution) and with
this solution wash the hair, and it will be black.

The Gaster Manuscript (Folio 128b)

'Ya, that is good!' The Countess Blythe Castiglione
snapped her fan shut, satisfied that Sia had solved her facial-
hair problem. Her quivering blue eyes looked shrewdly at
Will.

'Oh, Will, the project I have in mind for you is
tremendous. I want you to paint a portrait of me beside
the Navigator!' Her soft-cooking-apple face burst open
into a loud high-pitched laugh. 'Ya, I mean it.' She made
little patty-claps with her hands. 'Ah! look at your face, all
befuddled. You think I 'ave rollicked off the deep end and
have lost my wits completely.'

Will nodded that that was exactly what he thought, but
he wasn't serious; a smile wriggled under his lips.

'Ya, you think I care that much for the hoary old bastard? He left me, that was very aggravating. This festival may be in his honour,' the Countess Blythe Castiglione played with the beads dripping over her bosom, 'but the festival is just an excuse for distraction. We need something to prevent us from going mad, eh Will?'

Will looked serious now. Something the countess had said troubled him.

'Silas, my one true love.' The Countess patted her wedge of red hair and sharpened her tongue. 'I'd still break his neck if I saw him now. Pity the globe didn't smash his head.'

Isadora Elzbeth remembered the green globe at 30 Wexford Street.

'No, but Will!' the Countess stood up, her plump face and button-blue eyes glittering with excitement, 'when I say I want you to paint me beside the Navigator, I do not mean Silas the Mariner. Rather, I want you to paint me beside my most marvellous project to date.' She pointed out of the windows at the empty lake.

'Tomorrow morning. You will see. I shall say no more tonight.'

For a moment Blythe Castiglione stood silent, her fan clasped in her sausagy fingers, her layered face musing over something she was proud of. Then she extended her round arm, operatically whipped her fan open and squeezed out a slow tortuous note from somewhere deep inside her throat.

'Ohaieeeee aeee.' The Countess walked stiffly, her ample soprano figure heading for the window, her head turned sideways beseeching her audience with a pitiful array of sharp notes.

> 'The Navigator fell in love with me,
> He promised me his heart,
> Then in the dead of night,
> The scoundrel did depart.'

The song was farcical. The countess shrieked the high notes then rumbled into another verse which trebled her multiple chins as she turned full square, clasped her enormous bosom and boomed:

> 'The darkness it is on me,
> My one true love is gone,
> Into the caves of no return,
> Leaving my lonely heart
> To always burn.
> For ever is far too long.
> For ever is far too long.'

The last notes of the lament spiralled out into the room. The countess was genuinely moved. Her eyes disappeared behind her lids and her face scrunched up from the agony of trying to sing. An emotional tear plopped down her rouged cheek, and her Rubenesque body trembled as the last line died into a whisper before the silence.

Nobody moved. For a moment Blythe Castiglione stood with her eyes shut, frozen in her final emotional pose, with her hands extended, her fan and chins dangling and her lips pursed in a florid, fleshy roll.

'Of course, the music is Handel's!' The countess pounded her way back to the chaise-longue, and the delicate legs creaked as she flopped down weightily.

'I have composed the opera myself, telling the story of my romance with Silas. That what I sang was the last movement. Is it not astounding? You should hear the choir. The opera will be a display of lights and the costumes are pure white, representing the sea foam. Oh, it is marvellous. This is the best year ever, the most amazing Festival of the Navigator.' The countess grabbed Sia, whose mask now sat neatly on top of her head exposing her clear skin and pale eyes.

'Sia, darling, that is why I wanted the pearls so white, to sparkle with my wonderful costume. I have so many secrets this year. Wonderful, fabulous secrets. This opera will be remembered for many, many years to come.'

'What kind of secrets de ye have, Blythe darlin'?' Will asked, pinching a grape and throwing it into his mouth.

'Tomorrow you shall see one, in the caves. And then there are the women, two amazing musicians, that I discovered! Ya, look at your faces! It is the truth. They fell from the moon right down into my lap, and they will perform my opera with me!'

Sia looked at Isadora Elzbeth and Will looked at Sia.

'Two women who fell from the moon, is it? I suppose ye'll tell me ye believe in angels next?'

The countess rounded her shrewd eyes on Will, and her gingery eyebrows played see-saw as she wavered between telling him everything and giving nothing away.

179

'Ya, what if I do? There are plenty in Arcadia who swear they have seen the Archangel Gabriel.'

Isadora Elzbeth thought of the Darkman. She didn't care if he was an alchemist or an angel; all she cared about was the fact that Christina and Mrs. Buck were here, in Blythe Castiglione's villa. She wasn't alone.

'These women have the voices of angels. One is particularly good on the harpsichord, almost as good as myself. But I say too much. Tut, tut, it is your handsomeness, Will. How it disturbs my femininity and makes me want to tell you everything. You fabulous villain. Is he not disturbingly handsome, Sia?'

Sia blushed at the question, nodded awkwardly and fished around in her bag to hide her obvious embarrassment.

'I do nae believe ye, Blythe sweetheart.'

'No, it is true. After Silas, I declare you to be the most charming of men, with your long legs, and firm behind . . .'

'About the women,' Will interrupted, striding like a peacock towards the flirting countess.

'Oh, do you not?' The countess rose to the challenge. 'Well, you will see.' She thumped towards the door. 'I do not tell lies, well not all the time anyway. I . . . aha!' She swung round and waved her fan. 'I scold you, Will. You almost tricked me into showing you.' Will looked back innocently and shrugged his shoulders. 'You spin me like a top, round whirly-giggy round. I swear, it is because you are so handsome I get confused. Who are you?'

Isadora Elzbeth paled as the countess launched forwards

with all the interest of someone who'd just dug up a fat earthworm and was fascinated and repelled by it at the same time.

'I . . .' but Isadora Elzbeth couldn't speak. The countess walked around her and kept poking her with her fan.

'My new assistant,' Will said, coming to the rescue.

The countess was flabbergasted, her eyes bulging with disbelief. 'An assistant! An assistant!' She stared down at Isadora Elzbeth again.

'Aye, Blythe, an assistant. She's an orphan, from St. Paul's.'

The countess ripped the cushion cover off Isadora Elzbeth's hair and gasped.

'This is no orphan from St. Paul's. Look at her rippling hair.'

Panicked, Sia stepped forward. 'Do you like it, countess? I wanted to keep it as a surprise for you.'

'What?'

'I dyed her hair with the juice of fig leaves, jet black.'

The countess grabbed a clump of curls. 'Sia, you are marvellous, this hair is fantastic. Can you dye everyone in the choir's hair black too?'

'Yes, of course I can. Would you like your hair black?'

'Oh no, no. I will always have waspy-red hair. That is what Silas said he fell in love with first, my buzzy red hair.'

Sia delicately approached the next question. 'And these two women who fell from the moon, shall I dye their hair black?'

The countess frowned. 'This is a dilemma. Everyone

181

with black hair, and just me with red. Or everyone with black hair and three of us with different-coloured hair. Everyone, me, everyone, three, which is it to be?' The countess rolled the rhyme about for a while and finally decided that she'd think about it. Then she proceeded to stamp all over Will and Sia's feelings.

'So you are to be Will's new assistant? It is true you are pretty, but nothing of the gold of Marianne. You are trying to replace Marianne with this little darkling. What is your name then?'

'Isadora Elzbeth.'

'The girl with two names. Well, you know who I am? Blythe. Blythe by name and blithe by nature. Ya, is it not true, Will?'

Will looked cross. 'Aye, it's true, madam.' Then added sharply, 'If there is nothing more to discuss, I will retire. Shall I see you in the studio tomorrow?'

Oblivious to the hurt she'd caused, the countess shook her head and laughed. 'No. Not in the studio, in the caves. But you will see. Oh look, the party is moving out into the gardens.'

The guests emptied out of the music room and with flickering candles they drifted like spectres onto the lawns beside the lake.

'I must join them. I will see you all early in the morning. At sunrise. An old seadog like myself likes to rise with the first beams of the sun. You know your quarters. The darkling girl with the two names can stay in the room out there, fifth door on the right. So much to do

182

tomorrow. You have things to tell me, ya, Sia?' The countess winked, kicked open the French doors and called out, 'Yoo-hoo! Josephina, how do you feel about having black hair?'

She was gone, thundering across the lawn, barging her way into conversations and bullying her guests with orders and questions.

Will rolled his eyes to heaven and sighed. 'She'd try the patience of a saint.'

'They're here,' Isadora Elzbeth said. 'Christina and Marian are here, in the villa somewhere. We have to find them, they'll be worried sick.'

Sia stroked Isadora Elzbeth's hair. 'There will be no need to find them. We will be brought to them, probably tomorrow. It would make no difference going to them tonight. Will and I do not know the exact whereabouts of the ship, but tomorrow we shall.'

'I don't understand.' Isadora Elzbeth couldn't follow Sia's conversation. 'What ship?'

'The one the countess has been boasting about. The fabulous secret, somewhere in the caves. It's a ship.'

Will downed a glass of brandy. 'Of course, ye know her profession now. What was our famous 'Blythe by name blithe by nature' before she stole the title of Countess of Castiglione.'

Isadora Elzbeth looked out onto the lawn at the distant bulk of the countess weaving among her guests. It was hard to imagine what kind of job she may have had. Isadora Elzbeth had presumed that Blythe had inherited the title of countess, not stolen it. With this in mind she racked her brains, then she remembered 'an old sea dog like me likes to rise with the first beams of the sun'.

'She was a sailor.'

Will laughed. 'I knew ye were a bright little thing. She was more than a sailor, she was a famous cut-throat pirate in her day.'

Isadora Elzbeth was faintly shocked. She could see Blythe Castiglione as a pirate, with a purple patch over one eye and a brace of pistols at her waist and shouting orders to her crew, but cutting throats, that was a different matter.

Will pulled a chain from his pocket. 'I made ye a promise, lass, that if ye guessed her profession ye would be rewarded.' He undid the clasp of the delicate necklace. 'I was going to give it as a gift to someone else, but that was long ago. Ye've earned it.' Isadora Elzbeth recognised the entwined silver serpents that dangled from the chain. 'There,' Will said, stepping back, 'it looks well about yer neck. The silver catches in your eyes.'

Sia stood proudly smiling, and after a while she said, 'We should go to bed. All of us have an early start tomorrow.' Her expression slowly changed and she turned to Isadora Elzbeth. 'I don't mean to frighten you, but you must try to stay out of people's sight. You are in danger.'

Isadora Elzbeth removed her mask. 'How?' she whispered.

But Sia and Will looked at each other and in that look there was a silent pact.

'Do nae worry, lass, we'll get ye out of here. Ye and

Christina, Marian and Penguin. Now, let's away to bed. What room did the countess put ye in?'

They walked down the glittering corridor, counting the doors until they came to the fifth door on the right. Isadora Elzbeth stood with Penguin in her arms. 'This is it.'

'Good night. Don't worry, you're perfectly safe here.' Sia and Will kissed her cheek and Penguin's head to try and make her laugh before she went to bed, but it was useless. Isadora Elzbeth was deeply troubled. What was the secret that Will and Sia had? And where were Christina and Mrs. Buck? She said goodnight and waved Penguin's paw before opening the door into the dimly-lit room that the countess had directed her to sleep in.

A single candle stood in the window. By its weak light she saw that she had been put into some kind of storeroom, where boxes, crates, barrels and bottles were piled up. There was a table with dusty books, old sea charts and instruments. A love-letter lay rolled up, bound with purple ribbon, in one of the drawers. A trestle bed was against the wall. Over the dark fireplace hung an enormous portrait of a sailor with a thick red moustache, and, standing crookedly to one side, pointing out of the window at the moon, was the telescope from 30 Wexford Street.

'Oh, Penguin, they definitely are here, look.' She brought him to the window. 'The telescope.' She looked through the eye-piece, at the guests gliding around the edge of the lake. Then she swivelled the telescope upwards towards Cassiopeia and Pegasus, until it focused on the trailing comet.

'Look, Penguin,' she shoved his head against the eye-piece, 'a comet. Doesn't it look like a snake?'

'I'm bloody starving,' Penguin complained.

'I've no idea what it's called.' Isadora Elzbeth gave one last look at the orange trail beneath the moon. She squeaked with fright when the telescope slipped lower and she saw him standing on a distant tower, motionless as a statue, but definitely him.

'It's the Darkman.' Isadora Elzbeth shied back into the room, afraid that his deep eyes could penetrate the darkness and distinguish her across all that distance. 'Who is he, Penguin, and what does he want?'

'Sausages would be nice.'

Eighteen

To Make an Egg Fly in the Air
In the morning, prior to sunrise
Gather dew and fill with it an egg, and
Seal the hole well and put it against the
Sun and it will fly in the air.

Alchemical Writings of Hayyim Vital, No. 12 (Folio 79a)

Crack!

Isadora Elzbeth was woken up by a sharp smack across her face.

'Ow! Who? What?'

'It's a good way to wake up, ya! My mother always she wake me with a box in the ears. Toughened me up. Then one morning I was ready for her and I punched her in the face. That made us laugh!' Countess Blythe Castiglione let rip her ear-splitting laugh. She was dressed in a shock of purple-and-black taffeta, with an actual brace of pistols dangling below her waist. Isadora Elzbeth sat bolt upright and rubbed her eyes. 'Blythe by name and blithe by nature' definitely had a pair of pistols, pearl-encrusted ones, that slotted into ornate holders attached to a silver chain. Her hair was loose, fuzzing out in a wild anarchic bush down the length of her enormous back. She paced the room with her hands on her wide hips, her puffy face half-smiling.

'Ya, I miss my mother. Fabulous woman! Sold me to a sea captain when I vas twelve for two hundred florins. Very good with money. That was an excellent business venture on her part.'

Isadora Elzbeth wanted to laugh. 'She sold you?'

'Ya, well. I was a big girl, large appetite.' Blythe Castiglione's gigantic red head tilted to one side, she wore no make up today and because of this her eyes looked stronger, vinegar-blue with a glint of knife shining inside them.

'I knew how to look after myself pretty well. I could handle any man that tried to cross me. See these arms?' She clenched one arm until her muscles bulged up under the taffeta sleeves. 'Ya, you admire. I am a strong woman, could wrestle any man who bothered me.' She clumped towards the window and opened it up, a sharp wind gusted into the room. The countess inhaled, inflating her large bosom and throwing back her wild head.

'Ya. There are days when I imagine I can still smell the salt of the sea. The fresh, invigorating winds rippling over the oceans. The wide sky stretched overhead, the shrieking gulls tormenting the fish. And the flapping in the sails, the rigging clacking against the masts, the plash of the water lapping against the hull. The crew cursing, smashing open barrels of rancid meat. The burning taste of rum. The silence, just after we spotted another ship. How quietly we prowled after it, stalking it with blackened sails, creeping up on it in the dead of night. Then wham, flashes of gunfire, smoke, screaming, shouting, fighting, cannon blasts, swords drawn, pistols flaring.'

She turned around, her face and hair alive with electric memories. 'Then my blood would race, my heart would pitta-bam inside my chest, my brain would fizzle. Quick, quick, watch.'

Blythe Castiglione made stabbing gestures with an invisible sword. 'I was always big, but,' she held up one sausagy finger, 'I was always swift. Light on my feet.' Her hand dropped, her bosom heaved and she sighed. 'Ya, but those days are gone. Are you getting up? Sia has been out since before dawn. I saw her in the garden with a spoon collecting dew.'

Isadora Elzbeth nodded, patted Penguin out of the way and began to get dressed as Blythe Castiglione sat down by the dusty desk and looked about the room.

'It has been a long time since I was here last.' She rustled the old charts on the desk and one fell apart in her hands. 'A long time.' She pulled open a drawer and took out the love-letter bound with purple ribbon. She read it aloud.

You and I are from two different worlds, from two different times. But I swear to you, Blythe, I have never met a woman like you. You stir my blood, you have power, the force of a horse, the vigour of a tenacious dog, the strength of a lioness, the ferocity of a force-

ten gale. You are volcanic, a nagging toothache, a burst of over-ripe plums, a swell of treacherous waters, a spike of lightning. You are my one true love and I will always always carry you in my heart; no other could ever take your place. But I must return to my homeland, and you and I shall never meet again until we pass through the blackness and move on to the other side. I know you will stay loyal; I know my love will aggravate you until your very last breath. Every other woman that has ever roamed this earth, that lives and breathes now, is insipid compared to you. Your love is a nail in my heart, a black stone in my belly, a cloak over my lungs.

<blockquote>

Good-bye, my very own darling.
Your one true love,
Silas
aka Patrick James Seery

</blockquote>

Isadora Elzbeth couldn't move. Christina's uncle had been to Arcadia; she remembered a bedtime story Christina had told about her uncle dying. He had a Bavarian girlfriend. Blythe Castiglione! Things were falling into place. Perhaps it was no coincidence after all that she had fallen out of the balloon, perhaps she was destined to do so! Her head spun with the idea. She felt a strange comfort knowing that Christina's uncle had been to Arcadia and had returned home. He had got out of this time bubble and ended up back in the future. Isadora Elzbeth felt happy. She would go back to Ireland. She was going to be safe. She buttoned up her boots, smiling and glad, bursting to tell Will and Sia that everything would be all right, everything was going to be fine.

'Oh the bastard, the bastard.' Blythe Castiglione collapsed onto the table crying fat pitiful tears into her love letter. 'Still now he makes me cry. All these years his words can still scald my eyes. He loved me, and I have never known a love like it.' The countess stood up and walked towards the portrait of the sailor with the rusty-coloured moustache.

'So that is Silas?' Isadora Elzbeth stood beside the countess.

'Ya! Silas the Navigator.'

Blythe Castiglione rolled up the letter, twisted the purple ribbon around it and returned it to its place in the drawer.

'I cannot bear to look at it again. I cannot bear the pain,' she whispered. Then wiping away her tears, she said, 'We shall go to breakfast. I have rid the villa of all my servants, since I want the women to be a surprise. I can trust no one to keep the secret. So there is only us, Will, Sia, you and me, and the women of course. Come along, Issy Ellybit. What are your names again?'

'Isadora Elzbeth.'

'Ya, of course.'

The countess clumped her way down along corridors, through brightly-lit rooms, across luxurious halls, beneath smooth archways, until at last they turned into the breakfast room. Sia and Will were already there, Will drinking coffee, Sia arranging eggs in bowls by the window.

'Good morning, ladies.' Will rose and dipped his head.

'Morning, Will, Sia. I 'ave been getting to know your little assistant. She is like Marianne. She talks very little,

191

thinks a lot.' The countess tapped her temple. 'I'd say she thinks too much. So,' the countess flopped into her chair, which groaned under her weight, 'Ya, sit, Issy Ellybit. Let us gather round the table.'

Sia strolled over from the window. She looked positively beautiful today; her long brown hair poured richly over her shoulders, her pale moon-filled eyes had a soft hint of lavender about them. She smiled at Isadora Elzbeth, unaware that Will could not keep his eyes off her.

'There is so much to do today. The endeavour that I have hidden in the caves, do you know what it is?'

Will nodded.

'What do you mean, Ya? How could you know? It's been top secret.'

'It's been general knowledge, ye mean. Ye've built a ship.'

'What?' The question exploded around the room, and the countess bounded out of her chair and wrung her hands. 'So help me, I'll cut out all their tongues. Everyone from the helmsman to the carpenters. Are there no bloody secrets in Arcadia? Everybody bloody nosing in on everyone else, tongues waggy wagging, yap yap yapping. I was right to banish them all today, or else my other secret will become general knowledge, as you say.' Blythe Castiglione rolled her eyes to heaven and back. 'No one can be trusted.'

Discontented, the countess paced for a while, snorting and mulling things over in her mind. At last she looked shiftily, at first her right and then her left shoulder, as though she expected a new topic of conversation to be sitting on either one. Finally she turned to Sia and asked, 'Ya, Sia. You have found how to make the porcelain yet?'

Sia's compelling eyes looked brightly at a little wrapped bundle before her breakfast plate. She opened it up to reveal the polished shards of porcelain that had exploded in her kiln.

'You see. Milk ceramic.' She proudly handed a corner to the countess.

'Oh my goodness!' Blythe Castiglionc was flabbergasted. 'Ya, it is it. Oh, Sia, this is wonderful, this is so amazing. You have found how to do it. Oh my goodness.'

The countess flapped about in her shocking purple-and black-taffeta dress. She gasped at the shard, held it to the window, admired the milky light, spoke of its texture, its beauty.

'It is exquisite. After all these years, Sia, you have done it.'

Blythe Castiglione almost pounced on Sia to kiss and squeeze her, but she didn't. Sia was not the kind of woman to be pounced on or kissed at a whim.

'I haven't quite got the firing right.' She looked modestly at the broken pieces wrapped in paper.

'It'll nae be long until you do,' Will said softly, his face shy with admiration.

An egg floated across the table and everyone blinked.

'What?' the countess gulped. Another egg hovered wingless near her nose and another one bobbed towards Isadora Elzbeth.

Sia laughed. 'A little bit of fun for the festival. I found an old alchemical recipe to make eggs fly.'

She pointed towards the window, where two dozen eggs trembled in a bowl and one by one rose up and drifted eerily into the room. It was an amazing sight. Isadora Elzbeth walked into a clump of them and stood giggling as the eggs bobbed around her.

'It's magic,' she said. 'How did you do it, Sia, it's magic!'

The flying eggs made everyone's spirits light. Merrily they ate breakfast, while the eggs bumped and hovered around them. They laughed and talked and packed up equipment to take with them to the caves. They followed the countess out across the lawns to a boat on the lake. They giggled and wobbled getting into the boat and they fought over who was going to row. They sang a sea shanty, while Isadora Elzbeth told Penguin to leave the fish alone.

The countess and Will rowed.

'Ya, straight for the river, Will.'

They rowed over the lake into the river. Smoothly they wound their way through cornfields, along leafy banks, beneath trees, until at last the river narrowed into a deep ponderous channel that cut between steep sides. Dark trees hung down overhead, their branches twining into a tunnel. A hush fell over their good humour.

'The mouth of the cave is just ahead.' Even Blythe whispered now.

Sia began lighting candles. She quietly handed a few to

Isadora Elzbeth. 'Light these. There are lanterns behind you, light those as well.'

The entrance to the cave was a low, round opening covered in thick, hungry vegetation. The boat slipped out of daylight into a narrow claustrophobic tunnel of black dripping rock. The oars scraped against the sides. Isadora Elzbeth's heart pounded with tense expectation. She could see Sia's angular face half-lit by the candles, she could hear the dark waters sloshing. Every noise was amplified and heavy. For a long time they travelled the subterranean channel.

'Oh, my old arms, we must be nearly there,' said the countess.

'Where are we going?' Isadora Elzbeth whispered, uncomfortable with the darkness that folded around her.

'Into the caves beneath The Gate Mountains,' Sia explained. 'They say the inside of The Gate Mountains is just like Swiss cheese, a warren of tunnels and caves.' Sia reached for Isadora Elzbeth's hand and squeezed it reassuringly. 'They say if you are lucky and follow the correct river you will eventually get to the sea.'

'Ya! Or else forever wander in the darkness, looking for a way out, sailing forever nowhere, round and round.' The countess leaned towards Isadora Elzbeth. 'They say a thousand ships lie wrecked inside these mountain caves. Nothing left of the captains and crew, except what the rats did not eat!' The countess did not laugh. She heaved at the oars. 'Ya, but as I always say, who would want to leave paradise? Eh?' A semicircle of light appeared behind her, and the boat slid out of the tunnel into a wide, high, crystalline chamber, lit by three hundred torches.

'Wow!' Isadora Elzbeth's mouth fell open. It was like being inside a glacier. The jagged white walls glistened with magical hues. Stalactites met stalagmites, forming a legion of honeycombed columns that disappeared one behind the other into darkness. The water rounded out into a deep pool the colour of Caribbean blue. And there, amidst all this sparkling splendour, tethered by twelve ropes to a wooden pier, was a beautiful oak galleon with one hundred red sails and a carved mermaid at the helm.

'Ladies and gentleman, may I present *The Navigator*.'

The ship was a masterpiece of engineering, a carefully crafted vessel. Attention had been paid to every detail. The windows were fitted with small squares of glass, the masts were planed and strengthened with tar, and the rigging had been meticulously examined by Blythe Castiglione herself, every hoop, every pully, every twist of rope, all tested for strength.

'I'd take my hat off to ye, countess, if I had it on that is. It's a fine accomplishment.'

They disembarked onto the pier, and stood for a while just looking at the absurd reality of a galleon trapped inside a mountain cave, like a ship inside a bottle.

At last Will asked, 'What de ye plan to do with her?'

'This is where the second movement of the opera will take place. My stage,' the countess swept her roly-poly arm through the air, 'is it not magnificent? Ya? Well come on, take a look around, and then we will set up my position for my portrait. Ya?'

They climbed the narrow gangplank onto a gleaming ebony deck. Everything was sparkling new, polished to a high sheen. Penguin and Isadora Elzbeth wandered below deck. Every cabin was the same, furnished with red velvet, and each one had a porthole, and for a flicker of a moment Isadora Elzbeth remembered the ship inside the globe in 30 Wexford Street.

'I could see two ladies through the porthole window,' she told Penguin. 'Isn't it beginning to make sense to you? Well, not complete sense, but things are falling into place.' She sat down and played with strands of her hair. Above her she could hear the countess clumping around pointing out the extraordinary wonderfulness of it all.

'You will paint me here, at the helm, ya Will? Just like the sea captain I once was. Ya, where is your assistant, Issy Ellybit? What is her name again?' And she bellowed loud enough to wake the dead, 'Isadora Elzbeth, come along, we want to get started.'

Nineteen

The Supernal Serpent

The spiritus mundi (the spirit of the world) the supernal
serpent, the most lovely and also the most terrible,
who makes everything live, and also kills everything,
and takes on all shapes of nature.
In sum: he is everything and also nothing.

'Uraltes Chymisches Werk', by Abraham Eleazar 1735.

The Countess Blythe Castiglione stood on the upper
deck, looking over the balustrade, a spyglass in one hand a
sea chart in the other. Will stationed himself on the deck
below her, arranged his easel and ignored the countess as
she spoke down to him.

'Make me look impressive, Will, but maidenly. Strong
but fragile. I want to be lots of opposites. I want to look
like queen of the ocean, yet servant to the sea.'

The morning was lost in intense study. Isadora Elzbeth
helped Will mix his paints, and she watched carefully as he
prepared the canvas ground. With a mixture of turpentine
and blue oils he drew a shadowy impression of the countess

198

standing on her ship. His strokes were quick velvety swoops that looked nothing at first, until he began to apply red tones which suddenly fleshed the painting up. All the while Sia walked around the ship, scribbling something onto a piece of paper. Penguin followed her, hopeful that at some point food would turn up somewhere.

Late in the afternoon the countess produced a picnic lunch, most of which was fruit and salad, which disgusted Penguin so much that he wandered off in a huff.

'Fine,' he complained, 'I'll go native. I can be primitive too you know.' And for the rest of the afternoon he craned over the edge of the pool trying his best to snatch a fish out of the water.

All day Will painted. Sometimes the countess posed, other times she paced about telling stories.

'You know how I first came to play the harpsichord. It was when the Count of Saint-Germain came to visit Arcadia. You ever hear of him, Isadora Elzbeth?'

Isadora Elzbeth looked for Sia, but she was nowhere to be seen. 'Yes,' she answered.

'He was a fabulous liar, wasn't he, Will? Oh, but I better not talk to Will. The Count of Saint-Germain taught me how to play the harpsichord. He was a magnificent musician, involved in espionage you know. He was a spy!' Then her button-blue eyes flicked to Isadora Elzbeth, she smiled a teasing smile and winked.

'You know, Sia and the Count of Saint-Germain were deeply in love. It was rumoured they were going to marry. Is it not so, Will?'

Will's face was dipped towards his palette, but still Isadora Elzbeth could see he was furious. His mouth was a tight line, but although he opened it sharply his voice was controlled and steady. 'So they say.' He aggressively brushed a blob of purple onto the gown traced on the canvas.

'Ya,' the countess smirked, 'we all expected a day out. They were always disappearing off together. Eyes only for each other, staring at each other the live-long day. Everyone loved the count. Marianne particularly wanted her big sister to marry him. But then maybe she just wanted to get her big sister out of the way.' The countess looked pointedly at Will, but he ignored the sting of her remark and painted in the black stripes of her taffeta dress.

'Did you know that Marianne had an enormous crush on Will, Isadora Elzbeth? She was in love with him. They say Marianne was afraid her big sister would marry Will, so, when the Count of Saint-Germain came along, well, her problem was solved.'

Will looked up from his work. His face was thunderous. Isadora Elzbeth remembered how he had punched the guard, but he looked even more angry now. She stepped back, afraid of what he was going to say.

'Blythe, ye'r needling me with your remarks. Can ye keep still and fasten yer mouth?'

The words fizzled like acid on the air, but Blythe by name and blithe by nature, Countess of Castiglione, wasn't in the least put off.

'Now, Will, I am only repeating what was discussed by

200

so many people for so long. Do not be so angry. After all, it was long, long ago. The Count never married Sia, and Marianne has been buried for so many years do you not think it is time to declare yourself?' The countess steam-rolled over Will's feelings, mortifying his pride.

'She is an exotic-looking woman. So long you have this thing between you; perhaps it is time to forget the past, forget the count, forget Marianne, tell her . . .'

Will threw down his palette. 'Enough, Blythe, ye go too far.' Sia appeared from below deck just in time to hear him berate the countess.

'I will never forget Marianne, do ye hear me. I will never forget her.' His voice was strained, and a flush of red temper burned in his face. He caught sight of Sia from the corner of his eye and was suddenly silent. Although she smiled at him, it was a sad disappointed smile and Isadora Elzbeth figured it out for herself.

'*She* is in love with him, but she thinks *he* is in love with Marianne. And *he* is in love with *her*, but *he* thinks *she* is in love with the Count of Saint-Germain. How stupid.'

'Ya, Sia, there you are. Look at his artistic tempera-ment. He is magnificently masculine is he not?' The countess didn't seem to mind all the tension; in fact she looked as if she was enjoying herself.

'I cannae paint anymore today,' Will announced.

The journey back was quiet. The countess insisted that Sia and Will row the boat.

Isadora Elzbeth desperately wanted to see Christina and Mrs. Buck. She hoped once she found them that they

201

might be able to figure a way out of Arcadia. But nothing of the sort happened. Sia and the countess went into conference together, Will wandered off to be on his own and Isadora Elzbeth drifted through endless rooms with Penguin, hoping that somewhere she would stumble across Mrs. Buck and Christina.

'They're here in the villa,' she insisted, but after hours of walking through rooms and into cupboards, down to wine cellars and up to attics, without any success, she gave up.

'Oh this is useless, they could be anywhere.'

Penguin didn't care. 'I want pilchards or chocolate, or both. Feed me.'

Isadora Elzbeth stepped into the breakfast room, and an eggshell crunched under her feet. She found smoked sausages in the larder for Penguin, and he loved her so deeply for this that he let her carry him on her shoulders, all the way back to the storeroom where she had slept the night before.

'I'm fed up,' Isadora Elzbeth complained. 'Everyone has forgotten about me.' She lay down on the tiny trestle bed and fell asleep.

She woke up with a start. It was dark. The room was cold. It smelled of roses.

'At last you have come.'

The voice sent shivers down Isadora Elzbeth's spine. She turned stiffly and there, hovering near the door, was a girl she recognised.

'It was you,' Isadora Elzbeth whispered. She sat up

slowly. The ghost girl was the girl in the portrait over Sia's fireplace, the girl in Will's fresco, the girl in the mirror at 30 Wexford Street. Why did she only remember that now?

'You are Marianne Wish.'

Marianne glided nearer, her gold hair shimmering, her whispery voice crackling with joy.

'I am so glad you have come at last. I have been waiting for you for two hundred and thirty-three years.'

Isadora Elzbeth felt scared and she backed into the wall. 'That is a long time.'

'Oh please, do not be afraid. I will do you no harm.' Marianne's mint-green eyes winked with promises. She drifted nearer, her pale smooth face glowing with a waxy light. 'All this time and at last you are here.'

'You mean you were expecting me?' Isadora Elzbeth was perplexed by the predestiny of it all.

'I was expecting an agent,' Marianne explained, 'someone belonging to their own time, and I know you are it.'

Isadora Elzbeth thought of Russian war agents, police agents and spies. She shook her head. 'I'm terribly sorry, but I am not an agent. You see, I belong to another time, which I suppose is my own time, and I do have to get back there.' Then, remembering the Darkman, she said, 'But I think I know who you are looking for. There has been this Darkman following me. I think he must be your secret agent.'

Marianne laughed her ghostly laugh, as beads of rain splashed against the window. 'No,' she shook her corn-coloured hair, 'the Darkman is yours. You are the agent,

203

the catalyst for chemical change, you will undo what I have done.'

Isadora Elzbeth shook her head helplessly. 'I think you are mistaken. You see I have to go home, back into the future. I don't know anything about chemistry.'

'Back into the future.' Marianne moved to the window. 'You are mistaken, you are not in the past. I can show you, come and look at the sky.'

Isadora Elzbeth's head whirled with confusion, she wanted to say, 'Oh for God's sake, trust me, we don't wear clothes like this in the 1990s,' but she said nothing. Instead she walked to the window and looked at the sky.

'Do you see?' Marianne pointed just above the peaks of The Gate Mountains. For a while, Isadora Elzbeth saw nothing but a spattering of stars in the navy sky. Then she saw them, the pulsing red lights on either wing, the blue tail-light flashing on and off. In the distance, flying low over The Gate Mountains, was a Boeing 747.

'A plane!' Isadora Elzbeth gasped with astonishment. 'An aeroplane.'

Marianne's icy fingers glanced against her hand. 'You must listen to me, otherwise I shall have to wait another two hundred and thirty-three years for the python to return.'

Isadora Elzbeth was still reeling with the shock of discovering she had not gone back in time after all. 'What is all this about?' she asked desperately.

Marianne explained. 'In Arcadia, exactly two hundred and thirty-three years ago, a terrible sickness spread among the people. They got a horrible burning pox which began to putrefy and stink. They became black like pitch, and fell down suddenly. Chances were, if you entered a house where the plague had struck, there was no rescue. I lost my father to the disease, but I did not want to lose my beautiful sister. I worked night and day to find a cure. I slaved over fires, searched through the alchemical writings of the masters. Then I found it in Abraham Eleazar's work. '*Pater eius est Sol, Mater Luna, Vetus portavit in ventre suo.*' She spoke it like a prayer into the darkness.

Isadora Elzbeth shook her head. 'I do not understand Latin.'

'It means, "his father is the sun, his mother the moon, the wind carried it in his belly". It means that understanding comes with breath; knowledge is an inspiration, a breath.' Marianne struggled to make herself clear, but she was vague, and she laughed despondently. 'We alchemists have a saying, *I shall reveal a little and conceal twice as much*. I did not want my sister to die. I did not want Will to die. It was too late for me, for by then I was already showing symptoms.' She looked distracted for a moment. 'It was a remedy, a cure for the plague, that was all. They will never forgive me for what I have done.' She looked hopelessly into Isadora Elzbeth's eyes.

'Of course they will forgive you. What are you talking about? You stopped them getting a horrible sickness. What is there to forgive?'

Marianne wrung her hands, and her pale lips trembled. 'It was more than a remedy,' she said. 'You see it was the

Arcanum, the philosopher's stone.' Her voice shivered with dread. 'Immortality.' The word was a noose around Marianne's slender neck. 'I discovered how to make everyone in Arcadia immortal. Please, help me,' she begged. 'Please, you must help me undo what I have done.'

Isadora Elzbeth's mouth was dry, and she felt cold. 'What are you asking me?'

'They must die.' Marianne's whispery voice brushed gently against Isadora Elzbeth's cheek.

'You are asking me to kill them!'

Marianne pleaded, 'I am asking you to return them to the nature of things. Nothing more.'

The two girls looked at each other across the distance of two hundred and thirty-three years. A deep silence fell between them, until finally Marianne said, 'You are afraid, because your parents died and they are for ever silent to you now. You are afraid, because death is cold and lonely to you. But it is the chemistry of life, it is the moment of change, it is an engine. It is inevitable . . .'

Isadora Elzbeth sighed; she looked out into the night, into the deepness of space, and shook her head. 'Don't you see? I don't care what it is. I couldn't care less if death was a poem or a song. I don't care if it's nice and cosy. I don't like it. I do not like it.' She looked back at the ghost of a girl who had reached out to her over two centuries. 'I am sorry, Marianne. I cannot help you.'

Marianne covered her luminous face with her pale hands, and a single sob escaped between her delicate fingers. Isadora Elzbeth looked sadly out of the window and she wondered what it might be like to live for ever. She was sure she would like it.

'You wanted to know the secret between Will and Sia,' Marianne said. 'Now you know. They have lived too long. They want to make sure you escape, that you are not condemned to a multitude of wasted days like they are.'

'You are wrong,' Isadora Elzbeth said crossly. 'You are lonely, that's all. You just want them to die to keep you company.'

Marianne turned away defeated. 'I understand if you cannot do the task,' she sighed, and her sighs fell into the wind. She pressed no further, but sat on the window seat, despondent, looking out into the night, her ghost-white face resigned to the fact that she had failed. Isadora Elzbeth sat down beside her.

'I am very sorry, Marianne, but I told you I am no agent. I could not bear to harm Will or Sia. They are good people.'

Marianne nodded sorrowfully.

Isadora Elzbeth asked quietly, vaguely aware that someone was looking in at them from outside, 'What is it like being dead?' Marianne's reply unsettled her.

'I do not know. I am not dead, I am a reflection. I am a voice now. Nothing more than a Wish.' She pressed her hand against the glass and a man cried out in the garden.

Isadora Elzbeth jumped. 'Who is it?'

Marianne's voice was fading. 'They must expire. You must capture their breath, that is all. The comet is the python.' She pointed to the debris of glistening rock falling beneath the moon. 'It turns full circle, and comes back to earth every two hundred and thirty-three years. Gather the spirit of the python, mix it with the powder called "green apple", and let the wind carry it in its belly.' Her voice beat against the walls like the soft pahh of moths' wings. 'They are all condemned, but for the kindness in your heart.' Marianne's ghost was disappearing fast. 'Remember, "et in Arcadia ego".'

The light in her intense face hollowed out, her skin greyed, a bloom the colour of oxygen pushed underneath her features. She was turning into air. Like thawing ice, she melted slowly and all Isadora Elzbeth could do was watch her silk dress and golden hair dissolve like sugar in water.

Will burst into the room, wild with excitement. 'I . . .' He stumbled towards Isadora Elzbeth. 'I thought I saw, from the garden . . .' He looked hopelessly at Marianne's place on the window seat. He gathered his thoughts and sank down beside Isadora Elzbeth.

'Ye are alone, child.'

'Yes.'

Will looked downcast. His hawk-green eyes had lost their sharpness, and he slumped against the wall and sighed. 'A trick of light in the rain,' he murmured. 'I have been here too long.'

Isadora Elzbeth whispered, 'What do you mean, Will?'

He tried to shake off his depression. 'Ach, nothin', child. Only that the countess was right. We have to distract ourselves with something, otherwise we'd go mad, as crazed as the townsfolk.'

Sia came to the door holding a jar of bright-green chemicals. 'I heard a cry. I thought it was you.'

Will rubbed his face. 'Aye, going mad in my old age.'

'Are you all right?' Her soft voice twisted on a thread of fear.

Will's reply was kind. 'I won't lose my sanity, lass, not so long as ye are near.'

Sia came closer. She placed the jar on the table, kneeled down and gently lay her hand on Will's shoulder.

'You are tired, Will, you mustn't mind what the countess says. She's just whiling away her time.' Isadora Elzbeth backed into the shadows, melting into the darkness. She felt as though she were intruding.

Will cupped Sia's face in his hands and for a long time looked deep into her eyes. At last he said, 'Ye must find a way to undo what Marianne did.'

A tear trickled down Sia's cheek. 'I am afraid.'

Will comforted her. 'I will be with you.'

Sia cried heart-breaking tears and Will kissed every one.

'Hush, Sia darlin', do nae cry.'

'But . . .' she sobbed, and his mouth stole her breath with the gentlest kiss.

Twenty

'I don't care,' Isadora Elzbeth whispered to Penguin when Will and Sia had gone. 'I will not undo what Marianne has done. Besides, it has taken Will and Sia this long to get together. They need a bit of time to enjoy each other's company.'

'This stuff is glowing,' Penguin said, sniffing at the green chemical jar Sia had left on the table. 'The ghost girl had eyes like the stuff in this jar, pepperminty. This place is very odd,' he meowed.

Isadora Elzbeth sat down beside him. 'They can have all of eternity together, Will and Sia. It's very romantic.' She fingered the label glued to the jar and read the words, 'Green Apple'. For a while she stared at the malachite-coloured dust sealed behind the glass, and she could feel her heart sinking.

'Marianne said it was inevitable, Penguin.'

'There's something moving about in there.' Penguin tried to point to the gauzy green wings of something small flapping inside the chemical jar, but Isadora Elzbeth was preoccupied. It had stopped raining outside, and the clouds peeled back to reveal a rose-coloured new moon.

'Look at the moon, Penguin. Remember our nights by the river?' She opened up the window, only to witness Blythe Castiglione pushing a harpsichord out onto the lawn.

'Ya, come on. She will bring the brandy, you just help me push. God, how long have you been drinking? Stop whittering. Push.' Staggering beside the countess in her orange diamanté dress was none other than Mrs. Buck. A red-faced Christina streeled behind, trying to balance a decanter and three glasses on what looked like a mandolin case.

'No, no,' Blythe yelled, 'it has stopped raining, I tell you. Look, the clouds are departing. Now tomorrow the opera will begin here.' She pointed towards a lone cedar tree and bellowed, 'Push, Marian, what are you made of? Put your back into it.'

Mrs. Buck mumbled something into the harpsichord, turned around, leaned her back to the instrument and pushed. They heaved and puffed and panted until at last the harpsichord that had been in the oval music room was under the boughs of the cedar tree.

'At last!' Isadora Elzbeth squeezed her hands with delight, 'Penguin, they're here in the garden. Oh, what are you doing?'

Penguin had somehow managed to unscrew the lid of

211

the chemical jar. He had shoved his head inside and got stuck. He blinked out at Isadora Elzbeth and meowed rather pathetically.

'Come out,' Isadora Elzbeth said, trying to slide his furry head out, but it was stuck fast. Penguin struggled and wriggled, but it was useless.

He kept howling, 'I'm going to die with a jar on my head,' but the poignancy was lost on Isadora Elzbeth, who warned him she would have to get a hammer and smash the jar open if he didn't calm down.

'Penguin, we don't need this right now, I haven't got time. I want to see Marian and Christina.'

'I could suffocate. Don't leave me.' Penguin's meow was a high-pitched drawn-out whine.

Isadora Elzbeth carried him down into the garden with his head flattened against the inside of the jar.

'I promise I will free you,' she whispered, 'we just have to find the others.' The tinkling notes of the harpsichord twisted round the shrubs and over the lake. Suddenly, Isadora Elzbeth felt self-conscious. How was she going to present herself? Would she just walk across the lawns carrying Penguin with his head stuffed in a jar? Would she say hi! this is some adventure isn't it? She pushed through the shrubs until she caught a glimpse of the others. It was a fantastic sight. Mrs. Buck was sitting at the harpsichord, playing something beautiful. Christina was pouring brandy into enormous glasses, and the countess was lighting several candelabra, bellowing, 'Beautiful, beautiful. Play a little something by Scarlatti now.'

212

Mrs. Buck deftly ran her fingers over the keys and began playing a sonata. The countess was overcome. She ran out onto the lawn, flung her arms to heaven and began turning and dancing little butterfly steps. Her big womanly bulk twirled and jumped. Perhaps it was the music, or the trailing comet beneath the rose-coloured new moon, whatever it was Blythe Castiglione actually looked girlish dancing beneath the softly-lit sky. She fa-la-ed and pointed her toes, her ripe-apple face red with giddy exertion. Christina joined her, but she could only dance the flamenco. At last the two women collapsed onto the lawn. Mrs. Buck dipped her face into the huge brandy glass and sipped.

Isadora Elzbeth thought she might as well climb through the laurel bush that she had been hiding in.

It was Mrs. Buck who caught the first glimpse of her. One chocolate-brown eye peered suspiciously at her over the brandy glass. It blinked. She lowered the glass, stood up and marched forward, her face screwed up in some kind of fury. Isadora Elzbeth wanted to run in the opposite direction. Penguin panicked, 'Drop me, drop me, she's coming, drop me,' he howled. Isadora Elzbeth did drop him, the jar cracked open and the phosphorous-green contents scattered over the grass. Penguin ran.

Mrs. Buck was upon her. She grabbed Isadora Elzbeth by the shoulders and shook her hard.

'I won't have you haunting me, do you hear. I am sick to death of ghosts. Now go away to the other side and stop bothering me.' Isadora Elzbeth tried to wrench herself free, but tiny Mrs. Buck was strong as an ox. 'The girl with the golden hair, Gabriel and now you.' She suddenly let go of Isadora Elzbeth's shoulders and clutched at her heart. 'We didn't mean for you to die, it's absolutely awful.' Tears welled up, making Mrs. Buck's eyes look like chocolate-glazed cherries. 'You're dead right to come back and haunt us; we were careless. Oh poor Isadora Elzbeth, poor dead Isadora Elzbeth.' Mrs. Buck sank to the ground and wept.

'I'm not dead,' Isadora Elzbeth said sitting down too. 'I survived the fall, Marian.'

Mrs. Buck shook her head. 'You couldn't have. Poor, poor little Isadora Elzbeth doesn't even know she's dead,' Mrs. Buck cried into her hands. There was nothing for it, Isadora Elzbeth had to slap her face.

'OW.'

'It's to wake you up. Sorry, Marian, Blythe taught me how to do it. See, I'm not dead. You've never heard of a ghost smacking people on the face, have you?'

Mrs. Buck stroked her smarting cheek. 'But you can't have survived that fall.'

'I did.'

Mrs. Buck stared for two bewildering seconds, then she grabbed Isadora Elzbeth to her breast and cried all over her dark hair.

'You're alive, you're alive. I don't believe it.'

She sat clutching Isadora Elzbeth, rocking backwards and forwards and kissing the top of her head, until at last Isadora Elzbeth wriggled out, crying, 'I can't breathe, I need air.'

Then there was a delighted howl. 'Marian, Marian, is she with you? I see her too. She's come to haunt us. Thank God.' Christina crawled over the lawn, only faintly distracted by the phosphorus grass. 'Isadora Elzbeth, you have to know how sorry we are to have killed you. Marian doesn't think it qualifies as murder, but you were our responsibility, we should have strapped you into the balloon. You can haunt us until the day we die, we deserve it for our negligées, I mean negligence. We were stupid, stupid women.'

Christina was on all fours, her silver-grey hair tossed to one side of her head, her face flushed. Her chin puckered, as if she was going to cry. 'You're such a beautiful, tragic ghost. Isn't she Marian? Just like Cathy out of *Wuthering Heights*.' A bubble burst between Christina's lips and tears squirted out of her eyes. 'Oh Marian, remember the day she came to the flat and I said she looked like Cathy out of *Wuthering Heights*? It's like I cast a spell. I doomed the little darkling girl, and now she's dead. Poor, poor Isadora Elzbeth.' Christina was beside Mrs. Buck now. She flung her arm around her shoulder and cried, and Mrs. Buck joined in.

'And she fell through a cloud, Isadora Elzbeth did, down through the big deep clouds, down and down until . . .' Christina almost choked on her tears. 'Oh we are so sorry to have murdered you, aren't we, Marian?' Mrs. Buck shook her head.

'We are so.' Christina smacked Mrs. Buck's cheek to make her tell the truth.

'Ow, not again,' Mrs. Buck howled.

'You don't mind Marian. She is sorry. All we have been thinking about is your pale little face, and your long dark hair.' Christina reached for a curl and wound it around her finger. There she sat, her hand tangled in a dead girl's hair, weeping copiously. Every time Isadora Elzbeth went to say something, Christina burst out crying.

'I feel so guilty, you were such a little thing. But if it makes you feel any better, we are suffering. Aren't we Marian?'

Mrs. Buck was gingerly fingering her jaw. She nodded.

'We are lost. We can never return home. This place is so foreign and there's no way out.' Christina flapped her free hand and whispered loudly, 'They're all quite mad here. Crazy. With the birds. And,' she began to cry again, 'we're going to die here.' Then she howled miserably, 'We've gone back in time. We have been punished for killing you.' She tried to pull her finger out of Isadora Elzbeth's hair. She yanked at it and Isadora Elzbeth's head jerked forward.

'Ow, Christina. Take it easy.' Christina looked super-suspiciously into Isadora Elzbeth's face.

'Did you feel that?' she hissed incredulously.

'It hurt. If you wouldn't mind unravelling my hair . . .'

'But I thought ghosts were made of air, or that ecto-plasm mush thing.'

Isadora Elzbeth sighed. It had all turned out to be a bit tedious. Blythe Castiglione was snoring her head off on the lawn and Marian's attention was slipping in and out of focus. She was trying desperately to concentrate, mostly she was smiling vacantly. And Christina was obviously upset, her guilt pickled in brandy.

'I am not dead, Christina.'

'No you are, you're very dead, dead as a doornail.' She unwrapped her finger from Isadora Elzbeth's hair, held it up and began spouting poetry.

'Death be not proud,
Though some have called thee mighty and dreadful,
For thou art not so,
Die not poor death, since I am in the best of health.'

Christina's hand spread over her mouth. 'No, I don't think that's quite right.' Then she started on another poem.

'I met a traveller from an antique land

Who said –
Two vast and trunkless legs of stone
Stand in the desert.
So I told my father to rage, and rage
against the dying of the light.
Curse me, bless me now I pray,
Do not go gentle into that good night.
Because Ozymandias is there, and he is king of kings,
Look on my works, ye mighty, and despair.'

Christina laughed, a silvery little laugh. She pursed her lips coyly and whispered confidentially, 'I mixed up two poems there, one by Dylan Thomas the other by Shelley, or Keats, I always get those two mixed up. Oh, little Isadora Elzbeth, what is it like to be dead?'

Christina's hand flopped onto Isadora Elzbeth's dark curly head. 'Goodness, what a firm ghost you are.'

'I am not a ghost.'

'You're a fabulous ghost,' Christina contradicted, 'so pale and wistful. Tragic.'

'Tragic,' Mrs. Buck repeated.

'Tell her, Marian, tell her I am not dead,' Isadora Elzbeth pleaded.

'She's not dead,' Mrs. Buck unhelpfully repeated.

Christina wrung her hands and bit back more tears. '*Et in Arcadia ego*. Remember? Well that's you, your death in Arcadia.' Christina fell against Mrs. Buck. 'Oh we are hopeless adults, aren't we Marian. Look at what we did.'

Crack!

'Ow!' Christina wailed, 'why did you smack me?'

Mrs. Buck remarked sardonically, 'It's a trick that Blythe by name blithe by nature taught her. It's to wake you up, Christina. That's enough melodrama for one evening. The child is alive. Somehow, don't ask me how, she miraculously survived the fall.'

'But, but, all that distance to the earth, all that altitude, but . . .' Christina's forehead was a web of frowns. 'It cannot possibly be.'

'Well it is.' Mrs. Buck looked like she wanted to light up a cigarette; it was all too much nonsense for one lifetime.

Christina fell into a paroxysm of hugs and kisses, until finally Mrs. Buck wrenched Isadora Elzbeth out of her arms and told her to calm down.

218

'For God's sake, will you let the child breathe. You'll strangle her with affection.'

A short delighted silence fell over the three reunited friends, and the silence lengthened to a confused gap in the conversation that was at last broken by Mrs. Buck's rational opinion of events.

'We are delighted that you are alive, Isadora Elzbeth, but the point is we are still in a terrible mess. Somehow, we have gone back in time . . .'

'Which has been fascinating,' Christina interrupted. 'Some of their customs are quite barbaric. For example, do you know it is the custom for Arcadians to imprison travellers and keep them hidden. Blythe Castiglione has had us locked up practising her opera for days. We wanted to find your body to bring you home, but she refused to let us. Anyway, there is no way out of here. According to her the 'pass' is closed. You know, when we landed first, we thought we had happened upon a fancy dress party. It took us a while to realise we had gone back in time. I think, when Marian demanded to use the phone, that was the first hint.'

'The point is, we are now living in the eighteenth century and . . .'

'No we are not.' Isadora Elzbeth was firm.

Christina gasped in horror. 'Oh my God, don't tell me we're all dead and this is part of our after-life experience?'

Mrs. Buck tutted with annoyance. 'Will you leave death alone! What do you mean we are not living in the eighteenth century?' Mrs. Buck's sharp eyes flicked over the question.

219

Isadora Elzbeth gathered together the facts as they made sense to her. She showed them the flight paths low over The Gate Mountains. The women clutched each other's hands, delighted with the technological evidence.

'She's right, she's right,' they squealed, 'we're not mad.'

Mrs. Buck fumbled around her bosom and pulled out the butt-end of a French cigarette she had been saving for a special occasion; she stuck it in her mouth and stumbled towards one of the candelabra to light it. She returned in a haze of delicious smoke.

'So somehow,' she reasoned, 'this small country of Arcadia has remained insular protected by the mountain range from the modern world.'

'Isn't that fascinating?' Christina stood up. 'The community has continued the same customs and fashions that existed over two hundred years ago. Amazing, anthropologists will have a field day here.'

Mrs. Buck shook her head. 'And just how are they going to find out?'

The sad fact hit home, how were they going to leave Arcadia? Isadora Elzbeth stretched her legs and wondered where Penguin was. 'We can leave by *The Navigator*. It'll be risky though. If we take a wrong turn we could end up travelling underneath The Gate Mountains for ever, round and round, until the rats eat us.'

She told them about Uncle Silas. Christina insisted she wasn't shocked, that Silas was capable of anything. Though she and Mrs. Buck did talk at length about how strange it was that they should end up in Arcadia and meet the woman in the painting at 30 Wexford Street. They knitted the facts as they saw them together, and concluded after endless philosophising that they couldn't understand it.

'It's all very strange,' Mrs. Buck sighed. 'I feel like I am dreaming.'

Christina shook her silver-grey head. 'I'm afraid you're not dreaming. This is real all right, but, as Gabriel used to say, *reality is layered*.'

They bickered about Gabriel and his sayings for a while. Isadora Elzbeth only half-listened. She couldn't bring herself to tell them about Marianne, Sia and Will. She never mentioned alchemy or 'immortality'; somehow all those details belonged to another day. A sunny day. A day basking on the roof of 30 Wexford Street, safe and happy away from Arcadia and its ghosts.

Twenty-One

The path to immortality is hard, and only a few find it.
The rest await the Great Day when the wheels of the
universe shall be stopped and the immortal sparks shall
escape from the sheaths of substance. Woe unto those who wait,
for they must return again, unconscious and
unknowing, to the seed-ground of the stars, and await
a new beginning.

The Divine Pymander of Hermes Trismegistus

'**And just where do you think you are going?**'

Blythe Castiglione was standing with her two pistols pointed firmly at all three of them.

'You see what I mean?' Christina said. 'They're all mad here.'

'You were trying to escape.' Blythe Castiglione no longer looked girlish, she looked bullish. Her formidable figure strode towards them, and her flinty-blue eyes had a 'don't mess with me' expression.

'You were going to sneak into the caves and steal my ship. Back up.'

Mrs. Buck sucked on her cigarette, crushed the butt stylishly with her boot and calmly denied everything.

'No we were not. We were going to stroll by the lake.'

Blythe shot at her foot, and a cloud of powder circled the nozzle of the pistol. Mrs. Buck's mouth swung open with shock as the bullet lodged in the phosphorous grass. Blythe Castiglione had missed on purpose. The bullet was a message, 'a don't mess with me' message.

'Back up, all of you, including you, orphan girl. I don't care if you are Will's assistant or not. All of you, back inside the villa.'

Reluctantly they streamed back inside. Blythe pointed them down the glittery corridor and up sparkling stairways.

'Go on, go on. Stop trailing and traipsing. Up, up, and bring that stupid cat as well.'

Penguin poked his head out from behind an urn. 'Hi Christina, Marian.'

But neither women said hello, they just watched Isadora Elzbeth load him onto her shoulders.

'Keep going.' Blythe shook her pearly pistols threateningly. At last they arrived at a door that Blythe insisted they open.

'In here.' She pushed Christina who banged into Marian who fell over Isadora Elzbeth. 'Hurry up!'

The image of Blythe, Countess of Castiglione, as a cutthroat pirate made more sense to Isadora Elzbeth now. She opened the door and they filed into a dusty attic room. Blythe instructed them to light the candles.

'You will wait here until tomorrow evening, when I shall bring you your costumes and you shall perform my opera and, do not worry, you will be heavily disguised. Perfectly safe. I want this opera to go down in history, then we shall all depart together. Ya! That is right. Don't look so surprised. I too want to leave Arcadia. But we will go on my terms!'

Everyone greeted this astounding news with silence.

Blythe looked forlornly about the shabby room. 'I have been too long here, rotting away in splendour. For so long I have asked the question, 'Who would want to leave paradise?' And at last the answer is, 'I do.' Blythe looked sharply at Isadora Elzbeth, her button-blue eyes defiantly hard.

'I need the change,' she snapped. 'Don't look at me as if I were mad. I know what I am risking, little one. But I must go, I cannot bear another two hundred years of nothingness.' She backed out of the door, slammed it shut and locked it.

'You see what I mean?' Christina blurted out. 'Mad as hatters. *I cannot bear to live another two hundred years of nothingness.* What does she mean? And another interesting question, whatever did my uncle see in her?'

Mrs. Buck slumped into an old chair. 'Can't you sober up, Christina, we need a plan of action.'

Christina drew herself up tall, piqued by Mrs. Buck's remark. 'We *have* a plan of action. It just so happens that Blythe has now become part of it!'

Even Isadora Elzbeth had to concede that Christina was right. They would be sailing out of Arcadia tomorrow evening, with Blythe, Countess of Castiglione, captaining the ship. They sketched out how they thought the evening would run.

'The opera begins at twilight, beneath the cedar tree,' Christina told Isadora Elzbeth. 'All the cast will be in white, and everyone will have black hair except for us lot. Of course, you've already got black hair. Then the opera will glide on boats across the lake. There is a beautiful melancholic movement that will be sung in the candlelight as we head for the ship. The last movement will happen on board the ship. Then I presume the choir will be asked to disembark.'

Mrs. Buck disagreed here. 'No, I think the choir will sing from the pier and Blythe will perform her solo pieces on the helm of the ship.'

And so the argument raged, until both women got into a sulk about how the production was going to look. At last they fell asleep on some corn-filled sacks, leaving Isadora Elzbeth to wonder about everything. She stroked Penguin, who sat snugly curled up on her lap.

'I wonder what will happen to Sia and Will when we are gone, Penguin?' She imagined that they would be happy, despite what they had said to each other in her room.

'They can have all that time together, and Marianne can find someone else to undo what she has done.'

Then a strange thought occurred to her. 'Imagine, when I am an old, old woman, Will and Sia will be the same.' She dreamed of them working in the garden, or walking by the river, never changing, always young, always in each other's company, and that made her glad that she had not agreed to do what Marianne had asked.

Everyone slept.

Everyone woke.

They whiled away the day, until at last Blythe Castiglione burst through the door in a flurry of excitement.

'Ya! At last. Here are your costumes, ladies. I had to have one made specially for you, little Issy Ellybit.'

Blythe Castiglione looked remarkable. A swell of white silk bloomed all over her ample body. There were layers of skirts, a clenched bosom trapped in fine lace, puffy sleeves, dripping pearls, and a cloud of red hair frizzed out and speckled with rubies and precious gems. Now they could see what Uncle Silas admired about Blythe.

'Remember, it is vitally important you wear your masks. Should you be discovered, there is every likeli-hood . . .' She did not finish her sentence, but left it hanging like an empty noose. She patted her face, 'Oh my, I do believe I am a little nervous. All day, while you have been relaxing, the villa has been swarming with activity. It will be a wonderful show, a wonderful show, especially the finale.' She giggled and poked Mrs. Buck's ribs. Mrs. Buck scowled.

'Oh Marian, do not be cross; I had to imprison you to ensure you would not run off with my ship. You may as well forgive me. After all, we are to be travelling companions, all of us. I am so excited. Fast, fast, hurry up. The sun is lowering in the sky, and I wish the opera to begin at twilight.'

She waited impatiently while everyone changed into their immaculate white costumes.

'Ya, your masks, your masks,' she reminded them for the umpteenth time. 'So magnificent, all of you, worthy of a swan song.' Then she laughed her loud ear-piercing laugh and bellowed, 'Which of course is what it will be, a swan song! The last goodbye. But,' she rolled her lips and made an enormous 'shushing' noise, 'we will say nothing about our departure. Our secret, ya? Well, come along.'

Blythe jollied them down the stairs, along the corridors, and into a sumptuous dining-room lit by brilliant chandeliers. The choir had congregated there. Everyone was dressed in white, had jet-black hair and shell-white masks. Some practised singing in circles, others gossiped and sipped wine, while others tasted the minuscule delicacies piled high on ornate dishes. Mrs. Buck and Christina made straight for the food.

'God, I'm starving,' Christina admitted, as she loaded pastry after pastry into her mouth. Penguin managed to sneakily scrape some salmon down off the table. Blythe did her usual trick of hacking her way into conversations and burdening everyone with very specific orders which she kept changing her mind about. Isadora Elzbeth caught a glimpse of herself in a slender mirror framing the door. She didn't feel like it was her reflection. A pale-faced, masked girl with masses of dark curls and wearing a snow-white dress, just like a wedding dress, looked back into her eyes.

'That is me,' she told herself, 'the girl in the mirror.'

She watched Mrs. Buck and Christina eating and drinking. She wondered about the masked faces of the choir, whose eyes she noticed flicking over her. She began to feel uncomfortable. Everyone whispered when she passed by.

She wound her way through the crowd looking for Penguin, and found him staring out of the window.

'The sun is falling,' he whined. 'Is nothing ever going to stay the same?'

Isadora Elzbeth stroked his head. 'I'm afraid everything has to change,' she said intuitively guessing what Penguin might have said, and getting it almost right. 'Everything has changed for us,' she whispered, kissing his head. 'But we will return to Dublin tonight, and this whole adventure will be over. Nothing will ever be the same again,' she said sadly. Then she blinked. 'Oh yes! I see what you mean, Penguin. The grass is shining; that's where the chemicals fell last night.'

'No,' Penguin complained. 'The sun.'

Isadora Elzbeth nodded quietly. 'I see him too, Penguin. The Darkman is back.'

'Everyone! Hello, everyone. Ya! Thank you.' Blythe Castiglione clapped her hands for silence. 'I have been told that the guests are seated, the sun is sinking, the twilight is falling, the ambience is perfect. Has everyone their song sheets? Ya, good good. And their candles? Light up and get out. Ya. Go and arrange yourselves in a semicircle around the harpsichord, beneath the cedar tree. Go. Go!'

Isadora Elzbeth watched the choir file out. She

caught eyes looking at her, and one or two smiled nastily at her. She shivered, wondering why she should feel so uncomfortable.

Blythe bossed Christina and Mrs. Buck. 'No. Wait here, for God's sake. We have the grand entrance to make.' She circled the table, running loudly up and down the scales, and occasionally drawing breath to eat a finger of something dainty.

At last she deemed that a suitable amount of time had passed. Christina and Mrs. Buck nervously gulped down the liquid in their glasses and rearranged their masks.

'Our audience awaits,' Blythe shouted and in a flourish of white silk she swished out onto the lawn, with a faintly tipsy Mrs. Buck and Christina flouncing behind.

Three hundred guests rose and clapped their hands genteelly. Blythe twirled her hand at the appreciative crowd, and Mrs. Buck and Christina copied her. The crowd parted to allow the ladies access to the harpsichord, around which the choir had arranged itself in a half-moon.

No sooner had they arrived at the instrument than an enormous applause exploded. The guests cheered loudly, 'Hurray for the countess! Hurray.' Blythe bowed deeply and smiled a pained smile, loving every minute of it. At last she raised her plump hands for silence.

The crowd sank back into their seats, waiting to be transported by the music that was to follow. Isadora Elzbeth spotted Sia, a head above all the other women, sitting beside Will. She made her way through the rows of seated ladies and gentlemen, and quietly climbed onto Sia's knee.

'We ha'e been looking high-up and low-down for ye,' Will whispered urgently. 'Where ha'e ye been?'

'Blythe locked us up, but don't worry, everything is sorted.' Isadora Elzbeth noticed that Sia and Will were holding hands.

'What do ye mean "everything is sorted"? Ye're in grave danger.' He whispered the last words, looking worriedly about him.

Isadora Elzbeth couldn't understand what he meant. 'What are you talking about, Will?'

'Shh!' A lady in front hissed, 'the opera is starting.'

Will shook his head and watched anxiously as Marian began to play the first few notes of the opera. Blythe Castiglione stamped around the harpsichord. The choir hummed the first phrase so quietly that the notes mingled with the wind, and disappeared into the hazy twilight. At last the countess began to sing. A battery of off-key quavers tangled in the branches; her voice scratched over the tip of her fan and darted through the crowd; everyone squirmed in their seats. Christina stepped forward to sing a sweet alto harmony and ripple of whispers swept through the crowd. Isadora Elzbeth felt Sia tense up.

A man's voice cut through the music and interrupted the singing. 'She's not Arcadian. She's a stranger.'

The man stood pointing at Christina. Everything stopped dead.

'I don't recognise her. She's a stranger,' he bellowed, tearing through the crowd. He tried to grab Christina, who was so flabbergasted by the interruption that she stood mutely looking at the lunatic heading her way. Blythe Castiglione drew her pistol.

'Don't come one step further.'

The crowd gasped. The man stopped. Isadora Elzbeth tried to make sense of what was going on.

'You sit down in your place,' Blythe ordered vehemently. She waited, but the man did not turn.

'What are you going to do to me, countess? Kill me?!!!'

The audience burst out laughing. Blythe looked nervously at Christina, but it was too late. The man ripped her mask off and the crowd clapped furiously. Another man grabbed Mrs. Buck and tore her mask roughly from her face. Blythe fired at them, but the bullets were useless, the men could not die.

A woman stood up and shrieked at the top of her voice, 'Entertainment at last. Execute them! Execute them!'

The crowd surged forward, feverishly closing around Mrs. Buck and Christina.

'Dear God!' Will cried. He turned to Sia. 'Take the lass and put her on the lake,' he whispered. Then he battled his way through the taunting bodies, pulling men and women aside and shouting at the top of his voice, 'Ha'e ye lost yer wits completely?'

'Come on,' Sia whispered, but Isadora Elzbeth resisted. 'We can't go. We can't leave Marian and Christina, they'll be ripped apart.'

Sia dipped her head. 'He'll get them out. You have to be brought to safety, Isadora Elzbeth. Your only hope of

231

survival is the ship. Please, come now, before they notice you.'

Isadora Elzbeth didn't want to. She heard the crowd taunting and shouting. Blythe had been dragged to the ground and stamped on, while Christina was crying and clinging to Mrs. Buck. A woman jumped onto the harpsichord, screaming, 'Hack them open, crack their skulls, sever their heads.' She was such a pretty woman, with peachy skin. Will dragged her down and flung her to the ground. A group of men set upon him, and his cries for reason were lost in hysteria. At last the man who started the whole thing called for order. A rumble of excited silence fell over the savage crowd.

'Citizens,' he cried, with all the pomp of a self-important politician, 'it has been so long since we have witnessed a death.'

'Aye,' someone shouted, 'too long. Let's get on with it.' There were cheers.

'No!' the man shouted, and Isadora Elzbeth's heart fluttered with hope. She squeezed Sia's hand. 'Let us think about it.' The man's thin face twisted into an evil grin. 'I propose,' he announced maliciously, 'that we devise a slow death, to watch the life trickle out of them. Let us hang them by their pretty necks and watch them expire.'

The crowd cheered, then rushed forward. Christina and Mrs. Buck fought admirably, but it was useless. Sia tried to drag Isadora Elzbeth away.

'You must come,' she begged, 'otherwise the same fate will befall you.'

Two makeshift nooses of knotted lace and silk were tied to a cedar bough. Christina and Mrs. Buck struggled. Isadora Elzbeth felt herself screaming and running. She ripped her mask off. Sia was right behind her.

Isadora Elzbeth knew she was calling out for them to stop, but no one turned to look at her, no one heard her voice. All they heard was the ear-splitting whistle of the sky falling. Every head turned to look up. Coming at high speed from the east was a ball of molten fire, expelling sparks and cinders that fell in glittering, searing shards over the cornfields and woodlands. Fires broke out and bits of earth smouldered. The crowd stepped back, and still the asteroid rolled ever forward and downward, a streak of brilliant yellow in the twilight.

Isadora Elzbeth beckoned to Christina and Mrs. Buck. 'Come now,' she called, but they just saw her arm waving as they stole through the awestruck audience unnoticed. As Will marched behind them, a shower of grey ash fell hissing into the lake. The screech of the asteroid amplified, the yellowish glow of its arrival spreading out over everything.

They ran, all of them, including Blythe and Penguin, towards the rowing-boats in the lake. When Isadora Elzbeth looked back she saw the masked crowd running behind them, everyone's skin glowing with the colour of the yellow meteorite.

Feverishly they scrambled into the boats; Mrs. Buck, Christina, Penguin and herself in one boat, Will, Sia and Blythe in another.

The molten ball of fire crashed into a distant field. A loud explosion followed by a flare burst into the purple sky. A trail of gold sparks hailed down and scorched the grass. The Arcadians laughed at the passing danger and danced beneath the tongues of fire that fizzled down around them. Each flake of molten stardust burned brightly, before fading to ash on the lawns.

'We must row quickly,' Will ordered. 'They'll soon tire of the fallen star and want to see the spectacle of death instead.'

Christina whispered, 'Johannes,' with utter disbelief, but there was no time for conversation.

Then it happened. Isadora Elzbeth saw it. A wind that seemed to arrive from the furthermost shelf of the universe briskly stir the ash on the grass. She saw the chemical 'green apple' mingle with the stardust, and the wind flick and carry it like grey smoke up into the air.

She remembered Marianne's words; 'Gather the spirit of the python, mix it with green apple.'

'It was inevitable,' Isadora Elzbeth said, and her heart marvelled at how the inconsequential act of Penguin getting his head stuck in the chemical jar had made her undo what Marianne had done.

Christina and Mrs. Buck rowed frantically. Will, Blythe and Sia were already far ahead. They were beyond the lake, on the river, whose current dragged the boat swiftly towards the cave. They never saw what happened to the Arcadians. Only Isadora Elzbeth saw that.

The wind whirled the dust, carried it in its belly and

wrapped it round the ankles of the running Arcadians. The swirl of green-blue dust rose up, covering the silk costumes and powdered hair of the citizens and swallowing them whole. Isadora Elzbeth watched the grey-blue forms of what had once been. Now they were nothing but shadows inside a whirlwind. At last the dust blew so thickly that everyone was obliterated from Isadora Elzbeth's view. She heard a low moan beneath the howl of the wind. For a moment the air trembled with a melancholy cry. Then the ball of green-blue dust unravelled, moving visibly over the lawns, spreading out like a cape and heading towards the town.

They were gone. Not one Arcadian remained. Everyone had been spirited away. The trophies that proved that they had once existed now lay scattered on the grass. The scorched remains of lace cuffs and silk costumes fluttered eerily in the breeze. The lawns were littered with wigs and fans, old shoes and silver jewellery. Empty skirts billowed and rolled over empty jackets.

Nothing. Not one person was left.

'Like a nuclear wind,' Isadora Elzbeth thought. She shivered as she saw the distant wall of hazy-blue stardust making for the hillside, blotting out buildings, capturing the crazed inhabitants of Arcadia and reducing them to dust.

'It can't be like this,' Isadora Elzbeth reasoned, 'it can't have happened like this. I was supposed to mix things, and help, not do things by accident, against my will.' Furious that Marianne had got her own way, Isadora Elzbeth telepathically tried to summon up Marianne's ghost.

'I'll give her a piece of my mind,' she whispered.

'Look!' Christina's quivering hand pointed to a place beneath the drooping willow that fanned the bank. There, between the trailing branches, drifted the rowing-boat that the others had taken. It bobbed on the current, knocking against the green verge. It was empty.

'Where have they gone?' Christina wailed, utterly shocked. 'Have they drowned?'

They drew up beside the empty rowing-boat, and there inside it was Blythe Castiglione's white gown. Scattered round it were the bright jewels that had adorned her hair. Isadora Elzbeth wanted to cry when she saw the arm of Sia's dress entwined in the empty sleeve of Will's jacket, signifying their last embrace.

'*Et in Arcadia ego,*' Isadora Elzbeth said, resigned to the fact that somehow she had been responsible for all of this. She hugged Penguin close and turned her eyes away.

'We'd better hurry,' Mrs. Buck said, giving Christina one of her glares. Silently the women rowed into the cave. In the pitch black they made their way beneath The Gate Mountains until at last they arrived into the inner chamber where *The Navigator* lay moored.

'Dear God, it's amazing,' was all Christina could say, over and over again. They boarded the ebony decks, hoisted up the slender gangplank, untethered all the ropes. And stood hopelessly clutching the balustraded foredeck, admiring the sails that were pathetically useless inside the honeycombed cave.

After a while Christina whispered to Mrs. Buck, 'How

do you suppose they died?' But Mrs. Buck gave one of her fatal looks, which shut Christina up for five minutes at least.

'I don't suppose there's any kind of engine in this beast of a thing?' Christina blurted out at last. 'We're not going anywhere, are we? No engines in the eighteenth century now, were there?' She staved off despair by trying to work out just when the steam engine was invented. She discussed with Mrs. Buck how old wind-driven engines were. 'I think the Egyptians invented the windmill, or the Chinese. It is strange to think that the motor engine is so young really.' She eventually sighed, 'We're stuck, aren't we?'

The question hung over them, leaving them mute and without hope. Penguin shook his cat head and meowed, 'Of all the places to end up, beneath a chain of mountains with a gaggle of women! Such misfortune.'

'Shhh!' Mrs. Buck hissed suddenly. 'Did you hear that?'

'What?' Christina craned on her tippy-toes and looked through the layered columns that receded into the cave. 'Did you hear someone?' she queried breathlessly. 'Is there something there?'

Mrs. Buck looked darkly at the sails. 'Stop babbling, Christina. There it is.' She pointed to the pennant on the main mast. It ruffled. 'A breeze!'

A blast of hot wind suddenly billowed through the tunnels into the blue chamber, and each red sail filled up and puffed out. Everyone clutched the balustrade and

237

leaned into the sudden gust. *The Navigator* creaked, its enormous bulk slid forward and every timber groaned under the sudden movement.

'Get below deck,' Christina yelled, grabbing Isadora Elzbeth's hand and dragging her along. They fought against the gale and lost their footing as the ship banged noisily into the quartzite sides of the blue chamber. Mrs. Buck tumbled down the stairs. Christina promptly joined her, falling in a heap across her lap. Only Isadora Elzbeth and Penguin managed the descent below deck in an upright position.

The Navigator was cruising now. The wind roared furiously, pushing the ship forward, dragging it over humps of rock, pounding it past columns into pitch-black caves and along enormous arched tunnels that spanned miles of deep river. Below deck they spent ages trying to light a lantern without setting themselves ablaze. When lit, the lantern swung dangerously on its hook, throwing creepy shadows carelessly around the cabin.

The gale strengthened and every sail strained against its ferocity. Rigging snapped, somewhere glass shattered and something loud splintered overhead. Christina blanched; she remained very quiet. Mrs. Buck searched the cabin for tobacco. Isadora Elzbeth tried to peer out of the porthole. She saw a line of snow-white columns whiz by, then she saw nothing but her own reflection in the glass.

For hours the ship was pushed onward. Awful noises boomed and cracked all around them. The ship jerked and rocked, it twisted sideways, it straightened out. Christina clutched the table, and her knuckles gleamed white as every nerve in her body was strung out and stretched by the wind. Mrs. Buck raided the drinks cabinet and attempted to make a cocktail. Everything spilled and slopped as she tried to retain her balance. At last she handed everyone what should have been a 'Blue Mary', but in fact turned out to be a brown drink that tasted of molasses and rum. Everyone drank it, even Penguin. They tried singing over the wind, but being flung from one side of the cabin to the other didn't lend itself to singing.

Nobody knew how long they had been out there, but it was Isadora Elzbeth who spotted it. She dragged herself to the porthole and saw a fish, then a star, then bubbles, then a moon cloud, then a crab.

'We're on the sea,' she called.

Christina and Mrs. Buck clawed their way to the port-hole. *The Navigator* lurched upwards, riding a black wave, then it dived headlong down into the ocean and Mrs. Buck and Christina screamed as they and all the furniture were hurled forwards. The sea rolled up and over the edges of the deck, and white foam spewed as the ship sliced into the waves. Sails burst loose from their tethering, as the hull heaved under the strain of the black ocean. And all Isadora Elzbeth could do was remember the two ladies through the porthole of the ship inside the globe at 30 Wexford Street. She felt like laughing.

'We're going to sink,' she told Penguin, and the ear-splitting smash of the hull breaking apart proved that she was right.

⊚ Twenty-Two

The black hull struck a needle of rock. The timber sundered and splintered as the cold dark sea gushed inside. The ship rose vertically tossing everything downwards. Isadora Elzbeth and Penguin were flattened against a wall, Mrs. Buck and Christina came hurtling towards them followed by a gold chair and a writing table. There was another smash, the room split in half and the weight of the sea plunged in over them.

Everything vanished into a dark pressure.

Isadora Elzbeth couldn't scream, she saw the hem of Christina's dress flutter away into the darkness, and then nothing. She was dragged under and under, deeper into the airless ocean. The boom of every wave pounded fiercely in her ears. She felt her lungs suffocating, she stopped struggling, her smoke grey eyes blinked beneath the depths. She felt cold, overwhelmed.

His face was suddenly there, his dark eyes, black as pitch blinked at her, his bare muscular arms folded around her. She felt his strength plying the water, up through every dark rumbling wave, until at last they pierced the skin of the ocean and Isadora Elzbeth gasped for air. She leaned back, every breath hurt. Overhead the clouds ripped into thin shreds exposing myriad galaxies beyond the pale new moon. She saw the comet fall away beneath the horizon. The sea calmed into an undulating mass sparkling with starlight. Isadora Elzbeth splashed forward, she expected the Darkman to have vanished. But he was there beside her looking into the expansive night. She wrapped an arm around his shoulder, wanting desperately to keep him beside her.

'Who are you?' she finally asked.

He turned his eyes gently towards her.

'You know who I am.' He spoke with a faint accent, his petrol black hair gleamed, his taut face glistened moist with sea water.

Isadora Elzbeth smiled, 'I thought you were an alchemist.'

'I am,' the Darkman whispered.

'Then you are not an angel.'

The Darkman did not answer. He reached for her hands and held them gently, they buoyed silently in the water.

'I have gathered your grief and wrapped it around me,' he said kissing Isadora Elzbeth's forehead, she felt a heat travel to her heart.

'This is your time.'

He released her hands, she drifted from him. Hopelessly she tried to swim towards him. Suddenly the air trembled behind his shoulders. Two perfect crescents of silvery water swooped up and touched tip to tip behind him. They were wings. A film of prismatic light pulsed inside them.

'You will recognise me when we meet again,' he said, as he rose up out of the water in a hail of bright light. Isadora Elzbeth saw fire on the soles of his feet, he twisted into a blue flame. There was a blinding flash. He was gone, leaving nothing but a star burning in his wake.

'Come back,' Isadora Elzbeth called, 'I want to ask you a question.'

'There she is, there she is!'

Isadora Elzbeth turned around. On the shore was a swathe of lights. People were frantically running. There was a crowd. Something red billowed on the sand. Three men in luminous life jackets scrambled into a dinghy. She saw Mrs. Buck clutching Penguin and pointing into the sea. She saw Johannes Handley wrap a blanket around Christina, he kissed her and held her close.

'Hello Isadora Elzbeth, we thought we had lost you.' A man leaned out of the dinghy. He pulled her out of the water and wrapped her in a blanket.

Another man poured from a flask, 'hot chocolate,' he said. Isadora Elzbeth curled her blue fingers around the plastic mug and sipped quietly.

'You were a long time in the water,' the first man said, 'it's a wonder you're not dead.'

Isadora Elzbeth smiled, 'no, I'm not dead.'

242

Attic Press hopes you have enjoyed *Isadora Elzbeth*. To help us improve the series for you, please answer the following questions.

1. Why did you decide to buy this book? _____

_____

2. Did you enjoy the book? Why? _____

_____

3. Where did you buy it? _____

_____

4. What do you think of the cover? _____

_____

5. Have you ever read any other books in the Bright Sparks series?
   Which one(s)? _____

_____

_____

If there is not enough space for your answers on this coupon, please continue on a sheet of paper and attach it to the coupon. Post to Attic Press, Crawford Business Park, Crosses Green, Cork and we'll send you a Bright Sparks bookmark and catalogue.

Name _____

Address _____

_____

_____ Age _____

You can order your books by post, fax and phone direct from Attic Press, Crawford Business Park, Crosses Green, Cork. Tel 021 902980; Fax 021 315361; Email brightsparks@ucc.ie